I've travelled the world twice over,
Met the famous: saints and sinners,
Poets and artists, kings and queens,
Old stars and hopeful beginners,
I've been where no-one's been before,
Learned secrets from writers and cooks
All with one library ticket
To the wonderful world of books.

FAIR FRIDAY

On Fair Friday, the start of Glasgow's annual July holiday, a middle-aged un-ambitious journalist was fatally beaten up in a back court in a slum area. Fear of redundancy had driven him to a pathetic attempt at investigative reporting when he stumbled on a major scandal, which, in the eyes of someone highly placed in the underworld, necessitated his death. The case was handled by officers of P. Division and their investigation unfolds through the eyes of four policemen with different personalities, ambitions and techniques.

Books by Peter Turnbull
in the Ulverscroft Large Print Series:

DEEP AND CRISP AND EVEN
DEAD KNOCK
FAIR FRIDAY

PETER TURNBULL

FAIR FRIDAY

Complete and Unabridged

ULVERSCROFT
Leicester

First published in Great Britain 1983 by
Collins, London & Glasgow

First Ulverscroft Edition
published November 1984
by arrangement with
Collins, London & Glasgow
and St. Martin's Press. Inc., New York

British Library CIP Data

Turnbull, Peter
    Fair Friday.—Large print ed.
    Ulverscroft large print series: Mystery
    I. Title
    823'.914[F]   PR6070.U68

    ISBN 0-7089-1219-2

Published by
F. A. Thorpe (Publishing) Ltd.
Anstey, Leicestershire
Printed and bound in Great Britain by
T. J. Press (Padstow) Ltd., Padstow, Cornwall

1

TWO seconds after Bill McGarrigle realized he wasn't alone in the back court three of his ribs were busted. By the time he had rolled off the dustbins and on to the pile of garbage both his legs were broken, his skull was smashed and his attacker was in the street: just another guy going home.

He lay among the bricks and broken glass and tufts of stubborn grass until eleven o'clock the next morning when a wifie thought he was taking a bit long to sleep it off and so she went up to the corner and dialled three nines. He came to in Glasgow's Victoria Infirmary just before midnight, Thursday, nearly twenty-four hours after the sudden realization that the scraping noise wasn't made by any rat.

He opened his eyes and wished he hadn't: his head felt like what he reckoned Pearl Harbor must have felt like as the last Jap plane turned for home. He saw a dark figure rise and walk past him in the gloom, he couldn't feel his body, the only sensation was pain, big pain, sharp and penetrating, bursting from the middle of his head like a constantly exploding grenade. He couldn't hear anything: not even his own agonized groaning. Then another figure came and leant over him; he thought the second figure was very close but he couldn't see properly. He reckoned he was dead. He reckoned it had all come to this, gloom and fleeting figures and pain; the pain. It wasn't like they said it would be; it would be different from this, they said, different, fields and sun, happiness and green fields and different from this, not this, different from this, different . . .

"I should think he'll be out for another twelve hours," said nursing sister, withdrawing the syringe and wiping the swab across Bill McGarrigle's forearm.

"I really have to talk with him," said Phil Hamilton.

"No way." She smiled. "That uniform doesn't hold any sway in here. Anyway, you wouldn't have got anything from him, you heard him as well as me, he was rambling and in pain. He's better under sedation."

"Will he ever be able to talk?"

"Brain damage, you mean?" The sister looked down at the man on the bed, legs suspended on pulleys, head swathed in bandages. "Well, it's far too early to tell, he's certainly taken a crack across the side of his head, it's a messy fracture and there may well be bits of bone working into the grey stuff and that could cause complications. Most of the damage would have been done at the moment of impact and we won't know the extent of haemorrhaging for a few days. That will have to be soon enough for you."

"Aye," sighed Hamilton, and sank back on to the chair.

"What do you know about him?"

"I think he's a reporter, a newspaper man, on the *Clarion*. I don't know anything else."

"Well, somebody's got it in for him," she said in a nursing-sisterly voice, thin and clinical. "Smashed skull, broken legs, three broken ribs. There's more here than a regular closing-time square go."

"Looks like," replied Hamilton. "Reckon that's why I'm here. Wouldn't mind some more of your lovely hospital coffee in one of those lovely plastic cups."

3

"You know where the machine is, pal," she said, turning away. "Like I said, he's not going to say much for another twelve hours."

Thirteen hours later Bill McGarrigle started murmuring in his sleep. Constable Piper rose from the chair at the side of the bed and beckoned a nurse. He then went to the ward sister's cubicle and picked up the phone.

"He's coming round, sir," he said when he had negotiated the strange switchboard and was put through to D.I. Donoghue.

"Stay with him," replied Donoghue. "Someone will be right over. Take a note of anything he says." Donoghue put his phone down and walked smartly out of his office.

It took Richard King twenty-five minutes to negotiate the 1.00 p.m. Fair Friday rush hour and over to the south side. By the time he reached the hospital Bill McGarrigle was semi-conscious, he was groaning loudly, moving his head from side to side, swallowing hard yet still breathing shallowly. King sat on the chair next to the bed.

"Bill," he said. "Can you hear me, Bill?"

Bill McGarrigle nodded.

"Careful not to tire him," said the ward sister. The day ward sister was a good-looking woman of about thirty, fetching in a crisp blue and white uniform.

"I'll try not to," agreed King. "Is he with us, do you think?"

"Hard to tell," replied the sister. "Ask him his name or something but stop when I say so."

King turned to Bill McGarrigle. "Do you know your name?" he asked. Bill McGarrigle nodded but he remained silent.

"Your address, Bill," King pressed him. "What is your address?"

Bill McGarrigle's head was bandaged, he kept his eyes shut and swallowed hard, then whispered, "Langside, Cartside Street."

"Good man," said King. "Do you know where you are, Bill?"

"Flowers," whispered Bill McGarrigle. "No . . . flowers . . . no fields . . . sun . . ."

"He's rambling again," said the ward sister. "You'll have to stop."

"Possibly," replied King. "Possibly he's trying to communicate." He leaned forward. "You're in hospital, Bill," he said.

5

"Hospital," croaked Bill McGarrigle. "Alive?"

"Yes, Bill, you're alive, you're going to be OK."

Bill McGarrigle made a long low groaning sound and moved his head from side to side.

"I don't think he's ready for this," said the ward sister. "I'll have to ask you to stop now, immediately."

"Yes," nodded King. "Maybe we'd better leave it until he comes round properly." He sat back in the chair. "Whenever that's going to be. He could be out for days and the trail gets colder by the minute."

"He could be out for weeks," said the sister. "It's not unknown. And then he'll probably have a memory block."

"Comforting sort of person for a copper to have around, aren't you?" said King with a smile.

"Just don't want to build up your expectations of us being able to deliver you a perfect witness," replied the sister. "Now if you don't mind I've got work to do and I'm sure you have as well."

"Gilheaney," said Bill McGarrigle in a

6

voice like broken glass being swept up. "Gilheaney . . ."

"Gilheaney who, Bill?" King leant forward. "Gilheaney who?"

"Gilheaney," said Bill McGarrigle again. Then his head sagged backwards.

The sister leant forward and lifted Bill McGarrigle's eyelid and then took his pulse. "He's unconscious again. You couldn't have gone any further anyway, he wasn't up to it."

King stood. "Nobody's made any attempt to see him or enquire after him?"

"Only his wife," said the ward sister. "Why?"

"Just a thought," King said. "Somebody certainly wanted to harm him. I thought they might callously check on their handiwork or else come and finish the job."

"Well, no. Just his wife, like I said."

"Get-well cards already?" King nodded to the cabinet on the opposite side of the bed.

"Birthday cards," corrected the ward sister. "Brought up by his wife last night. He's forty-seven today."

"Many happy returns, Bill," said King.

7

King drove the short distance from the Victoria Infirmary to Langside. It was a snug part of the city, squat, solid-packed tenements, respectable working-class folk, aspiring middle classes, single people at the bottom of the housing ladder with a room and kitchen. There were corner shops run by industrious Asian families, but a two-mile hike to the nearest bar.

Mary McGarrigle was an ashen-faced woman. She sank back deeply into an armchair by the fireplace after having insisted on standing when King entered the room.

"Police, Mother," said the second woman in the room. King thought she was nineteen, she had mousy hair, was on the plump side of a full figure, and King reckoned she thought she was attractive. Mary McGarrigle stared at the fireplace, the brass ornaments, the decorative tiles, the picture of the Queen, summer holiday postcards sent from friends and relatives.

"She doesn't know where she is," said the younger woman to King.

"Uh-huh" King grunted. "Has she said anything about where your dad was going on Wednesday night, love?"

The girl shook her head.

"And you don't know what he was doing?"

The girl sank to her knees by the side of her mother's chair and grasped her mother's arm. "Mum, can you hear me, Mum?"

Mary McGarrigle nodded.

"Where did dad say he was away to Wednesday night? Can you remember, Mum?"

The woman shook her head slightly. Her eyes were wide, and she didn't blink. She just stared into the hearth, zombie-like, watching some drama played out on the tiles.

"Do you know, love?" asked King. "Any indication would help."

"No." The girl shook her head and stood, but kept a hand on her mother's shoulder. "Sometimes Dad would be out late at night, working. He's a reporter, you know." There was pride in the girl's voice. "But he shouldn't have been out late. They were to be packing last night."

"Packing?"

"For their holiday. They had the two weeks booked at Rimini. Dad can take his leave at any time, but Mum likes to go away during the Fair. Her family go back a long way in Glasgow and to go on holiday any time but the last fortnight in July doesn't seem right to her."

"Reckon I feel the same," said King, more to himself than her. Then: "You're not going with them?"

"They aren't going either now, but no, I wasn't to go with them. They wanted me to right enough, but we spend enough time arguing at home without doing it in Italy as well."

"Who, you and your dad?"

"No, me and her." She nodded down at her mother.

"Can't quite see that."

"Well, it's a bit different the now, isn't it?" She patted her mother's shoulder. "Sometimes, most times, we scream at each other enough to raise the roof."

"You got on all right with your dad, aye?"

"Aye, he's dead quiet in the house. When me and her start up he just pulls on his carpet slippers and pads into the kitchen."

"Quiet sort of bloke, is he?"

"Och, aye. He takes a pint now and again, but most of his free time is spent in the house. He has a wee study where he writes his articles or reads his books."

"So it was unusual for him to be out late at night?"

"Unless he was working. Then he'd phone and tell us."

"But he didn't phone you on Wednesday night?"

"No. We expected him back at seven to start the packing. They always pack two days before the flight."

"You didn't report him missing until Thursday morning, though."

"Well, what do you think the police would have said if we told them a middle-aged, intelligent, responsible man hadn't come home for his tea and it's nine o'clock already. Come on!"

"Nine o'clock was when you started to worry, aye?"

"Nine o'clock was when we knew something was up. You could set your watch by him. He didn't do any—what's it called?—" she waved a fleshy hand in circles—"investigative journalism, the sort that keeps reporters out all night. He worked late hours sometimes but they were predictably late, if you see what I mean."

"Was he working on anything at the moment?"

"I don't know. He didn't talk a deal about his work."

"Never mentioned anybody called Gilheaney?"

"Gil . . .?"

"Heaney, Gilheaney, ever heard him mention that name?"

The girl shook her head.

"And you've no idea what he was doing in Rutherglen?"

"None. Like I said, Mr. King, he never talked much about his day-to-day work. But it must have been his job that took him there."

"How's that?"

"Well, we have no relatives in Rutherglen and he has no friends who live there. None that I know of, anyway."

"OK," said King, edging towards the door. "If you think of anything that you think may be important, you'll let us know?"

The girl nodded.

"Be visiting him tonight, then?"

"Yes. We've got some gifts to take, and some more birthday cards arrived this morning." She nodded at the table on which were two gift-wrapped parcels and a small pile of envelopes. "We'd be going anyway, of course."

"Best drink of the day, this one." The man drained the glass and ordered another drink. "Make it a double, chief," he shouted at the barman in the red shirt and black bow tie. "You were lucky to catch me, son. Sure you won't have one?"

"Sure," said King.

"Yeah, I can usually knock off at five-thirty, got kept back late by that derailment. We wrote it up and processed the pics and it'll be in the early edition, hit the streets at midnight. You heard our slogan: 'Buy tomorrow's *Clarion* today'? You know what our circulation is, son? Close on a million. Not bad, not bad at all, that figure, all over Scotland and Northern England and a big batch to Corby. Do you know Corby, Northants? It's a little Scottish town right in the middle of England? Sort of an outpost."

"It's not so little," said King.

"You've been there?"

"Once or twice."

"So that's why this is the best drink of the day. Our work is fast, blood pressure way up there, so at five-thirty I drink a shot or two of whisky to unwind. More if it's been a busy day. I'm killing myself, forty-nine already, overweight, don't take exercise, smoke like a decayed taxi-cab, but what a way to go. Newspapers, son, can't beat it as a way of life. Smoke, son?"

King shook his head. He had been standing at the commissionaire's desk in the foyer of the six-storey concrete and glass *Clarion* building. The commissionaire, a long thin man, picked up the phone and dialled. He stopped as the lift doors opened at the side of his desk. "Here he is, sir," he said in a high-pitched voice. "Mr. Ralston, Detective-Constable King to speak to you, sir."

Outside it was a muggy afternoon, a light grey blanket of high cloud covered the city and wouldn't let it breathe properly. Ralston jerked his tie knot loose and unbuttoned his shirt collar. He carried his jacket under his arm. They gave a couple of drunks a wide berth.

"First of the many," said Ralston, stepping into the gutter. King noticed fat rippling across the man's stomach under his silk shirt. "Reckon you boys will be busy tonight?"

"Usually are," said King.

"Going away for the Fair, son?"

"No."

Ralston took him to the Big Deal near Charing Cross. "Makes me feel young," he said, "these new bars, bright colours, bright lights, and the girls, the girls, you should see the girls that come in here. I don't get on in the old bars, son, take themselves too seriously, just wine and spirit and no women. They haven't any spirit, if you see what I mean. Two whiskies, chief. Big ones."

"Tomato juice," said King.

Ralston grunted a grudging concession, but insisted they stay near the bar. "Something to lean on," he explained.

"Bill McGarrigle," King prompted as Ralston took delivery of his second hit.

"Oh yes, Bill McGarrigle, cheers, son. Nice bloke, Bill McGarrigle, been with the paper for ten, twelve years. Sort of makes up the numbers on the office outing rather than being an ace reporter. That's his problem."

"In what way?"

"Times are hard, son, the paper's cutting back on costs. We're losing sales. We even put our topless lovelies in colour and clawed back a few sales, then lost them again, so we made them as near bottomless as we dared—that worked for a bit but sales are dropping again. We print a lot of paper but we also carry a lot of overheads and we aren't making a lot of profit. I don't know the ins and outs, I'm just a sub-editor, but the *Clarion* has a wee bit put by to enable it to sail through the lean periods, only this lean period is going on a bit too long. That's where Bill McGarrigle comes in, or goes out."

"I don't follow."

"Simple, son. If the paper can't survive by boosting sales it's got to survive by cutting costs. The Board's been laying down some heavy restrictions, you should see my car mileage allowance, it's now half of what it was last year. Another whisky, chief, one for the Fair, and a tomato juice. Hurts me to order a fit young man a drink like that."

"Duty," said King.

"Or diet, eh, son. Could do with losing a couple of pounds here and there, couldn't you? Don't tell me I can talk, son, I'm not bothered. Here we are, one tomato juice, uh!"

"Bill McGarrigle," said King drily. "You were saying?"

"About Bill, yes, hell of a nice bloke, Bill. Family man. I'm a family man, but not like Bill, always for his family, Bill is. You know the type, don't give a sod about promotion, offer him overtime and it's like you're offering him a dose of clap. But being a nice bloke doesn't keep you in work. Bill has no nose for a story. He has to be told what to do like he was a trainee. I'd say go out and cover the Bathgate Beautiful Baby competition and away he'd go, happy as a sandboy because he'd got something to do. He'd take all day over it, would Bill, and come back and write his two hundred words and then putter off home in his VW. See, son, there's another reporter on my staff, a whizz kid, he's not just high flying, he's in the stratosphere already, he sniffed out a real scandal: some building being closed down by the Local Authority, boarded up, I mean, locked and shuttered. Nothing wrong with that, you might think, but it turns out that the mindless neds in the city hall are

17

shelling out thirty thousand quid to redecorate the place before turning the final key. Can you believe it, son? That's ratepayers' money, our pennies. We exposed it and they shut the place without a paint and paper job. Anyway, the bright boy hunted that story down by himself and brought me the complete piece before I even knew what he was working on. Some kid. We got good mileage out of it, you know: 'Where does our money go?' And we found a big hall in the south side packed to the rafters with sports equipment and enough musical instruments to equip three orchestras, all good stuff, violins, harps, thousands of pounds' worth. Turns out it has all been accumulated over the years as one department spent up in order to get its full whack each April. And guess what?"

"Never used," said King.

"Gathering dust and cobwebs, and in this city of all places." Ralston drained his glass. "In the end we stopped the investigation because the pattern of local government spending is so stupid that it was making the readers depressed. But the point is that when staff have got to go, who do you chop, the whizz kids or the Bill McGarrigles?"

"I see," said King. Then: "Let me get you one."

"Lovely, son. Double, *s'il vous plaît.*"

King edged into the bar and caught the barman's attention quickly enough so as not to disgrace himself in front of Ralston.

"Cheers, son," said Ralston, clutching the glass which King thrust at him. "No, it wasn't the chop, not the straight chop. Bill's put a lot of time into the paper and so I had a couple of words with him, but I didn't pull any punches. I told him I needed hard news from him and on his own initiative. He had to produce, I told him, or we'd let him go."

"How did he take that?"

"Much as you'd expect, or rather much as I would have expected: shaken not stirred, if you see what I mean."

"I don't."

"Well, son, it came as a bit of a shock to him to learn that he was vulnerable. I think as the years had ticked off he had come to think that he was like one of these Local Authority eejits we discussed earlier. You know—high on a no-redundancy index-linked pension kick. He went home a bit white-faced that day but I can't say we got any excess action from him after that."

"Still the same?"

"As far as I could tell. Did once tell me he was on to something big, need a few days to work on it, Dave, calls me 'Dave', does Bill. Didn't say what it was, wouldn't say, pressed him but he wouldn't give. All he said was that it was something big in the city, but he didn't seem to be working harder, just the same Bill, plodding about watering the plants and sharpening pencils."

"When was this?"

"Last Friday. A week ago today and that was two weeks after I'd had that talk with him."

"And you had no idea what he was working on?"

"Like I said, son, he wanted to give it to me gift-wrapped, a *fait accompli*."

"No idea why he was in Rutherglen?"

"None."

"The name Gilheaney mean anything to you?"

"No, no, can't say it does, son. You could check his papers, if he'll let you go through

20

his desk, and there's also his diary and his notebook. If it's OK by him it's OK by us."

"I'll ask him," said King. "When he comes round."

"Still out, is he?"

"I was wondering if you were going to ask after him."

"Now, son, don't spoil a good Fair Friday bevvy by getting nasty. I am interested in Bill, I gave to the collection we had for him today, but it's been a hard day for me."

"Sure," said King.

"I would've visited him tonight but it's a family affair and anyway there's a committee meeting at the golf club. Which reminds me, I'd better shoot. Take that for me, will you, son?" He pushed his empty glass into King's hand and forced his way through the crowd in the general direction of the door.

King placed both glasses on the bar and weaved his way out of the pub. He walked the few hundred yards to where "P" Division police station stood, on Sauchiehall Street, at Charing Cross, just west of the Motorway.

It was a hot, close evening. King's shirt stuck to his back with sweat. The doors and windows of the bars were flung wide and the punters spilled on to the street.

It was Fair Friday, the eve of the day each year when Glaswegians quit the city for their holiday, flying to the Mediterranean resorts and latterly to Miami, or more traditionally to the northern English resorts which they hold like an army of occupation. The original fair had long since gone but the last two weeks in July retained a significance without which Glasgow just would not be Glasgow, and a stranger walking down Sauchiehall Street on Fair Friday night would be forgiven for thinking that the entire city was smashed.

King entered the police station, nodded to the desk sergeant and signed in. He had signed on duty at 7.00 a.m. that morning and it was now 7.00 p.m. Four hours of unavoidable overtime, but then that was no new experience, not for a policeman in this city. He walked up the stairs to the first floor and the CID rooms and hung his jacket on the stand next to his desk. Montgomerie was at his own desk, leaning back in his chair reading the *Evening Times*.

"How," he said without lowering the paper.

"How what?" asked King, sinking into his chair and looking across his desk and reading the paper's headline. FAIR HEATWAVE!

"White man speaks with forked tongue," mumbled Montgomerie, turning the page of the newspaper.

"Give me peace, Mal." King rested his head on his arms, folded across the desk. "I can't take your sense of humour, not right now."

"Chief Medicine Man Fabian wishes to see white man in teepee for heap big Pow Wow."

"At least I'll get some sense from him. When does he want to see me?"

"Messenger say as soon as white man comes in from hunting ground."

King pulled himself to his feet, grabbed his jacket and walked along the corridor to Fabian Donoghue's office. The door was shut. King slipped on his jacket, made sure his artificial knotted tie was clipped on properly and tapped the door, twice, just below the sign, "Inspector Donoghue".

"Come in," said Donoghue.

King pushed the door open and entered Donoghue's office. Donoghue sat forward resting his forearms on his desk, a tall man in his early forties. He wore a waistcoat with a gold hunter's chain looped across the front and his University tie was pushed firmly up to his collar. His one concession to the heat was that he had taken off his jacket and it now hung neatly in the corner of his office. His pipe was in a large glass ashtray on the right of his desk, and in front of his hands was a sheet of paper. Ray Sussock sat in a chair in front of Donoghue's desk.

"Ah, King," said Donoghue as King stood just inside the doorway. "Excuse me, Ray."

Ray Sussock grunted.

"The assault on Bill McGarrigle, you're handling it, I understand?"

"Yes, sir," said King.

"We had a message from the Victoria Infirmary while you were out." Donoghue patted the sheet of paper on his desk with his palm. "He died at six-ten this evening. It's a murder enquiry now."

"We haven't . . . I haven't dug up much to go on, sir. One name. Gilheaney. He said that while he was semi-conscious so it may or may not be relevant. It has no significance to his family or place of work. Also, no one knows how he came to be in Rutherglen. What's certain is that he was working on something but no one knows what."

"All right. We'll meet in my office tomorrow at eight-thirty a.m. sharp. The trail's still hot so it'll mean weekend work for us all. That includes you, Ray."

"Fine by me, sir," said Sussock diplomatically, because nothing could be further from the truth. His suitcase was packed, the delectable Elka Willems was waiting for him in her small flat in Langside, they had rented a holiday cottage near Mallaig for Saturday, Sunday and Fair Monday. There was the possibility that Elka Willems, being a policewoman, might understand when Sussock arrived home and said, "I'm sorry, love, but . . ." Sussock conceded that it was highly unlikely, but the remote possibility remained that she would agree to give up her break and spend the weekend in Glasgow. "Fine," he said again.

"Montgomerie in, is he?"

"Yes, sir," replied King. "He's writing up in our office."

"Ask him to come along here, please. Then you'd better get home and get some

25

rest, you look like you could use it. You too, Ray."

Ray Sussock left the police station with his jacket under his arm, his tie in his pocket and his shirt collar open. He wanted to look as unlike a policeman as possible because right then he didn't want to be a cop. He was a Glaswegian by birth and spirit and at fifty-four he was old enough to feel the real significance of the Fair. He was old enough to remember the long queues at the railway stations and the boats taking the folk down the water to Dunoon and Rothesay. He could recall the signs chalked on the boards at the factory gates and the entrances to the shipyards: "Hooters to the Fair—3." "Hooters to the Fair—2." "Hooters to the Fair—1." And he liked to get away for the Fair, even if it was only for the Fair weekend. To get out of Glasgow, to be part of the great exodus was the thing. He walked up Sauchiehall Street and took the tube from Buchanan Street to Hillhead. He walked from Byres Road to his bedsitter looking as much like a slob as he could, because he wasn't a slob, he was a cop who wasn't to get away this Fair because some guy had got his skull smashed open in a back court in Rutherglen.

27

2

THE summers in west central Scotland are rich. They are rich in lush vegetation and rich in humidity, and the combination of both can, in the evenings, for a few weeks each year, suggest a sub-tropical climate. They are also rich in daylight, enjoying a midnight sun effect when, for a brief period at the solstice, the darkness is nothing more than a deep twilight, reaching its most dim at about 3.00 a.m., by which time it's getting light again. By Fair Friday it was still warm enough in the evening for a group of men to work in their shirtsleeves, and it was still light enough for them to start a two-hour search. The men were police officers and they were searching a back court in Rutherglen. It was 7.30 p.m.

The police officers swept the uneven surface of the back court, the coarse grass, the broken glass, and waste-bins. They were not slow to attract attention and shortly after the search commenced scores of faces peered down from the tenements into the backs. The other source of attention came from the mosquitoes, and the policemen spent as much time slapping forearms and scratching scalps as they did sifting through garbage and turning over stones. Fabian Donoghue stood in a closemouth, supervising the sweep while working hard at maintaining a strong smokescreen with his pipe to keep the insects at bay.

While the backs were being searched Malcolm Montgomerie questioned the people who lived in the block. It was an old tenement, well over a hundred years old and most likely the original development on its site. None of the 120 flats had a bath, though some had a shower. The toilets stood where the stairs turned below each landing, one toilet for three flats. The frames on the stair windows were rotten and about to fall away from the wall. In some cases they had fallen, leaving great gaping holes through which Montgomerie could see the new school beyond the backs and the railway at the side of the tenement. Some flats had been abandoned and the doors sheeted over with corrugated iron. One or two of the iron sheets had been pulled away, revealing a black cavity, smelling of glue and cheap wine turned to vinegar. But it did seem a dry block. He was still suffering from shock at discovering this aspect of the city: until he put on a uniform his reality had been the smugness of Bearsden and the self-satisfaction of the Faculty of Law at Edinburgh University.

He pressed the bell or rapped the knocker of each door he came to. Eight times out of ten the door was opened, usually by a woman since most of the men were in the bars. Montgomerie knew the content of most interviews before he rapped on the door:

"Good evening. Police. We're making enquiries about the attack which took place in the backs here on Wednesday night . . ."

"I didn't see nothing."

"Nothing at all?"

"No."

"The attack took place about midnight, perhaps a little later."

"I was in my bed/bevvied/out until three/night shift."

"You didn't hear anything, a shout perhaps?"

"No. Nothing."

"If you do hear anything will you let us know."

"Aye."

"Thank you."

"You're welcome."

Most times Montgomerie was right. Most times. In the fifth close, three up, was a solid, brown-painted door. It hadn't got a name plate, but a foreign name which Montgomerie could not pronounce, Jaruduski, had been printed in large capitals on the plaster at the side of the door. There was a large arrow pointing from the name to the door, which had a heavy metal knocker. Montgomerie rapped it smartly.

It was opened slowly and then only by six inches, being held on to the frame by three safety-chains, all heavy duty and, it seemed to Montgomerie, to be homemade adaptations rather than the delicate bronze apparatus which could be purchased in hardware shops. The face that peered out at him from a square formed by the door, the frame, and two of the chains, was a face Montgomerie had seen before. But not in the flesh. Thank God, not in the flesh, but in the newspapers, on the television, looking at him from behind barbed wire, or glancing

31

at the camera as he ran from Soviet tanks. It was a long thin face with sunken cheeks, piercing eyes deep in their sockets, and a scalp shaved close to the skull.

"Police," said Montgomerie.

"Polizie, ha!" The man started to push the door shut but Montgomerie held it open. "Polizie!" said the man again. There was an unmistakable note of alarm in his voice.

"It's OK," said Montgomerie calmly, trying to assuage the terror he saw in the man's eyes. "I just want to ask you some questions."

"Kestions!" The man had a piercing voice. He kept his long bony fingers wrapped round the door, his fingernails were splintered and bitten down. "What kestions you have?"

"About the attack in the back court, two nights ago."

"I seen it. Timofei see it."

"You see it!" said Montgomerie, involuntarily slipping into the man's broken English. "I mean, you saw it?"

"Ja. Not good ha! You go polizie. Not good."

"What did you see, Mr. Jar . . ."

"Yaroodooski," said the man.

"Mr. Jaruduski," Montgomerie repeated. "What did you see?"

"Ah, ah! Not good. Go, go. Night falls. I have to shut door. Go."

"No," said Montgomerie firmly. "You have to tell me. If you want to shut the door then let me in and shut it behind me."

The man stared intently at Montgomerie for a few seconds and then nodded. He shut the door, slipped off the chains and then opened the door again. The man's flat was unlit and the curtains were drawn shut so that Montgomerie had difficulty in making out objects in the gloom. As he entered the flat he noticed a bunch of garlic hanging by the door frame. Timofei Jaruduski shut the door quickly behind Montgomerie and threw a heavy bolt across it. "Will do until you go," he said.

Montgomerie thought it probably would do; the bolt sounded heavy enough to be of use in the Bank of Scotland.

The living-room was sparsely furnished, the air was musty and stale but also suffered from an overpowering smell of garlic. Montgomerie went across the odd scraps of carpet and pulled the curtain back to glance down the street. He couldn't see anything clearly because the glass was thick with grime. He noticed that garlic had been crushed and smeared on the inside window-sill and around the window-frames.

"Expecting visitors?" he asked, letting the curtain fall back.

"They come. Each night they come."

"Each night?"

"Oh yes. Believe me. When the night falls they come."

"Like last Wednesday?"

"Yes. Last Wednesday. I saw him."

"You were outside?"

"No. I never go out at night. It is not safe. I saw him from the window."

"How could you?" Montgomerie said shortly. "You can hardly see the building across the street through those windows."

"Timofei can. Sit, sit, Polizie, sit."

Montgomerie peered into the gloom and made out the dim shape of a sofa. He fancied if it was a shade lighter he would be able to make out little things hopping from cushion to cushion. He said he'd prefer to stand and then asked again about Wednesday night.

"I see him all right. Big, big."

"Where did you see him?"

"Out there." The man indicated the front window.

"No you didn't," said Montgomerie. "It's almost still broad bloody daylight and I can't see a thing, so how is it you can see something at the dead of night?"

"Timofei can. I show you." He grabbed Montgomerie's arm and dragged him to the left-hand corner of the window. It was a bay-window which protruded from the side of the building with the side panes of glass at ninety degrees to the wall. Low down on the side window-pane was a small area of glass which was kept clean. The curtain was held away from this part of the window, which also attracted a larger than usual pile of garlic. "My spy hole," he said with pride.

"You have one on the other side too?" Montgomerie turned and came face to face with heavy and dusty curtains.

"No need. Look out of my spy hole and tell me what you see."

Montgomerie obliged. "I see up the street," he said.

"So. Now look at the windows opposite."

"My God, I see what you mean," said Montgomerie softly. In the bay-window side panes of the house opposite he could see the reflection of the street extending down towards the bridge across the railway.

"At night it's even clearer," said Jaruduski. "Here I keep watch."

"And you saw one on Wednesday night?" Montgomerie stood and faced the man and noticed for the first time how tall and well built he was by comparison to Jaruduski.

"Ja. So you are too a believer. There are so many who do not believe. Who cannot see."

"Tell me about the sighting?" Montgomerie ducked Jaruduski's question.

"He came out of a close, further down from this close, and he flew down the street. He kept near to the building. At the bridge he dropped something on the line and then disappeared into the night. It was a strong sighting. I have not had many so strong."

"You did not see the attack?"

"No. I heard about it from the kind lady across the stair who brings me my food each morning before I go to my bed."

"Stay up all night, do you, Mr. Jaruduski?"

"All night, watching. I have many

sightings but rarely as strong as the sighting on Wednesday night."

"You should turn your light on. They don't go for lights."

"I couldn't pay the bill and they took my meter away. That was ten years ago and I have used candles from then. Now you must go, there is still time before night comes."

Montgomerie located Donoghue in a close. He was pulling furiously on his pipe. "They're getting immune," he said as Montgomerie approached.

"Perhaps they're flying underneath your smokescreen, sir."

"Whatever it is, they're coming in thick and fast." He slapped the side of his neck.

"They're females," said Montgomerie. "They're sucking your blood to nourish their eggs."

"I don't wish to know that, Montgomerie."

"Speaking of which, sir, I've just met an odd-ball two closes away. I think he saw the attacker running away. There was no description worth taking down but he did indicate that something may have been chucked over the railway bridge."

"Well, what have you done?"

"Nothing, I . . ."

"Well, get on with it, man. Take Piper with you, you'll need to corroborate the finding of any evidence. Piper!" Donoghue summoned the constable and then sucked and blew on his pipe. Mosquitoes danced crazily in the smoke. "What do you mean by no description worth taking? What sort of investigation is this?"

"How about leathery wings?" said Montgomerie, moving his arms slowly up and down.

"Get on with it!" snapped Donoghue, and turned to watch the progress of the search.

Constable Piper took a transparent Cellophane bag from the boot of the area car and followed Montgomerie towards the railway bridge. They stood at the parapet and looked down on to the rails.

"What are we looking for?" asked Piper.

"Probably the murder weapon," replied Montgomerie, trying to scan the four tracks which seemed at that height in the fading light to be one wide band of varying shades of grey.

"We're not going to see it from up here."

Piper stood back and looked at the embankment on either side of the bridge.

They chose to scramble down the steep embankment on the left of the bridge, and Montgomerie walked the width of the tracks while Piper stood at the side keeping a lookout for trains. Five minutes after Montgomerie had started the search he stopped and knelt down between the rails. Then he looked up and beckoned to Piper. Piper glanced up and down the track and then joined Montgomerie.

"Looks good enough," he said, and handed Montgomerie the Cellophane bag.

Montgomerie had found a length of heavy metal pipe, about two feet long with matted hair and congealed blood stuck to one end.

"This is one I'd like to see through to the end," said Piper as he joined Montgomerie at the top of the embankment.

"Join the club," replied Montgomerie, brushing dry soil and parched blades of grass from his trousers. "There may be a big motive behind this attack."

"Besides that," said Piper, "I was there when they pulled the sheet over his head and sent for the concealment trolley. I've seen dead people before and I've put people in ambulances who didn't last out the ride but I've never been there when the Grim Reaper arrived."

"Does that make a difference?"

"Yes. Shouldn't it?"

"No," said Montgomerie, turning back towards the tenement block. "Don't get involved. Let yourself get involved in this work and you're finished. How old are you, Piper?"

"Twenty-two, sir."

"Yeah, well, I'm twenty-six and I'm telling you it's a job like any other and we can't let our feelings get in the way of our doing it. We may find out there's no motive after all and he was knocked over in an argument after a trip to the gin bin."

"No, I don't feel that. I saw the guy, I saw his family and the get-well cards. Going into the back courts rat-arsed pissed at midnight wasn't his style."

"How the hell do you know, Mr. bloody twenty-two-year-old Police Constable Piper?"

"I saw the guy, like I said," replied Piper calmly.

"You don't know what's ahead of you, Piper. You can't imagine the people you'll

40

find stacked up against walls in gin alley with puke dribbling out of the corners of their mouths. You name them, Piper, and I've seen them, company directors, doctors, teachers, solicitors and newspaper men. They all get bevvied and they all find a space on the wall or a vacant stretch in the gutter. Most of them have families and most receive get-well cards and we have to treat them all the same. Detachment, that's the word. Stay detached or you'll take it all home with you."

"There's more than that here," persisted Piper. "I have this intuition."

"We'll find out soon enough," said Montgomerie wearily, "but I'm telling you."

They reported to Donoghue, who they found had taken to pacing up and down the close to assist his pipe smoke in fending off the mosquitoes. He stopped walking as Montgomerie and Piper approached him and stared intently at the two officers.

"Length of metal, sir," said Piper. "Accretions at one end which may be blood and human hair."

Donoghue continued to stare.

"Found on the railway line, sir,"

stammered Piper. "By DC Montgomerie. I witnessed the find."

Donoghue grunted. "Take it straight down to Forensic, please, and ask them for an immediate report." Piper left the close, Donoghue and Montgomerie looked at each other. "Carry on," said Donoghue.

"Sir?"

"The rest of the flats in the block, Montgomerie, carry on."

"There are six more closes, sir," Montgomerie protested. "Can I have assistance?"

"No. Let me know when you're finished. It's only another sixty or seventy flats." He tapped the ash from his pipe against the wall and hurriedly refilled it. "And don't forget to call back on any flats which are empty tonight. Everybody who lives in this block must be interviewed."

"Very good, sir," said Montgomerie, turning away.

"Oh, and, Montgomerie . . ."

"Sir."

"I'd be pleased to see a little more gravity in your approach to your work. I like dignity and seriousness of mind in my officers, and I like a sense of humour in its proper place.

This is a profession, you know." Montgomerie started to reply but Donoghue's face was suddenly hidden behind a flickering flame from a gold-plated lighter and a blast of blue smoke.

Montgomerie, chastened, worked his way up each close, progressing along the block towards Rutherglen Main Street. As he worked he found that the frequency of blocked-up doors increased, the stench in the closes got stronger and the people on whose doors he rapped were increasingly drunk. In the hundred-plus years of its existence the block had developed a "good" and a "bad" end. He stepped over remains of fires, tramps' dosses, and piles of beer cans and spoke to punters who were too drunk to realize who he was but who insisted on shaking his hand before he left their door.

But it was for this that he had quit the Law. He thought that you had to be here at this level; if you could take this, then you earned the luxuries in life simply because you could appreciate them. He believed deeply that if he couldn't take one, then he shouldn't accept the other. In Edinburgh the law students wanted to be advocates;

they had starched white collars, learned quickly how to sniff wine and called their clients "the Jimmies". He finished his degree and returned to Glasgow to plumb the depths of his native city, searching for his own level. If in the process he laughed, then he felt it wasn't entirely out of flippancy.

He walked out of the last close at ten-thirty. Donoghue and the other officers had long since left. In his notebook was a list of twenty-seven flats from which he had received no response to his knock and which would have to be revisited. It was a warm night, the air was still, the first few drunks were staggering out of the bars. Montgomerie glanced up at the block and saw the drawn skull of Timofei Jaruduski at his spy hole. Montgomerie raised a hand in greeting and the face recoiled into the gloom.

3

BY 9.00 a.m. on Fair Saturday the sun was hot and high, the sky was blue and cloudless, heat hazes hung over the roads, the girls in bikinis were stretched out on the grass in the Botanic Gardens, the kids sucked on ices and the oldies rolled up their sleeves. The city was hot and windless, baking, shimmering, glistening.

Ray Sussock jerked on the handbrake as he stopped the car outside the *Clarion*'s multi-storey complex. The beads of sweat trickled off his brow, his stomach hung heavy, and his shirt stuck to the small of his back. He would normally have walked the few hundred yards from "P" Division to the *Clarion*'s offices on the waterfront, but he was angry at losing the Fair weekend so he drove, gunning the engine. It would not be so bad if she had stayed, but last night after she had thrown the teacup at the wall she stated that she was not staying in Glasgow during the Fair weekend, no way, old

Sussock, not even for you and Fabian bloody Donoghue. She'd be up there now in the holiday cottage, probably cycling to the beach with her blonde hair flowing behind her and her swimsuit under her T-shirt and jeans. She'd even managed to get him out of bed early to drive her in a car borrowed from the Department to Queen Street Station in good time for the 6.00 a.m. to Fort William. He slammed the car door and stormed up to the commissionaire's desk in the foyer of the *Clarion* building, showed his I/D and said, "Bill McGarrigle, I want to see his desk."

The Commissionaire was about sixty, with thin-lensed spectacles and greying hair. He turned Sussock's I/D over in his hand and slid it back across the desk top. He lifted the telephone and spoke into it, listened, replaced the receiver and said, "Floor five, sir." He nodded to the twin lift shafts beside his desk. On the fifth floor Sussock was met by a second commissionaire, younger and more rotund than the first. Sussock followed him down a brightly painted corridor with a parquet floor.

"Some bad luck, eh?" said the

Commissionaire, holding a door open for Sussock.

"About Bill McGarrigle?"

"Working during Fair weekend," said the Commissionaire with a grin. Sussock noticed he had a brace on his lower teeth. "Still, someone's got to do it. We take turn and turn about. I'll get the September weekend off. It's not so bad working holidays so long as you get plenty of notice. I suppose it's the same in your job . . ."

Sussock didn't reply.

"Mr. McGarrigle you're interested in, sir?"

"His desk, specifically," replied Sussock as they entered a large room with big steel desks arranged in rows. Each desk had a telephone, some had two, and all had wire baskets containing assorted sheets of paper. There was a large calendar on one wall and on the other side of the room the window ran the length of the office, giving an impressive vista of the city's central business district, the tall buildings of the finance houses, the banks, the insurance companies and the oil companies. All silent and empty.

"This is Mr. McGarrigle's desk, sir," said the commissionaire stopping by a desk on the left-hand side of the room, about half way down. There were a few other people in the room who glanced up curiously at Sussock.

"You're not the only one to have to work, then," said Sussock.

"That's what I said," replied the commissionaire. "We keep a skeleton staff in case a big story breaks. You should see it on a weekday, messengers running, people shouting into phones, rush hour eight hours a day. How is Mr. McGarrigle, sir?"

"You haven't heard?"

"I haven't, no, sir. I don't think anybody has."

"I dare say you'll find out soon enough," said Sussock quietly, pulling at the drawers of the desk and finding them locked. He felt for the key on the inside of the desk, and then began to rummage among the plants and pads and stationery. He lifted the blotter and finally looked at the commissionaire. "Key?" he said.

"Key?"

"Key."

"Ah," said the commissionaire.

"You don't have a spare key?"

"I'm afraid not, sir." The commissionaire

looked uncomfortable. "The Administrative Officer might have a spare, but . . ."

"He's away for the holiday and his office is locked."

"Yes, sir. How did you know?"

"Happens all the time," said Sussock drily. "You object if I fiddle with the lock?"

"Can you open it without a key, sir?"

"With your permission, but I won't be able to lock it again."

"Well, I don't know, sir." The commissionaire stammered and looked round, keenly aware of the handful of people in the room. "I'll have to take advice."

"Don't bother," replied Sussock, already straightening a paperclip. "You can say the police pressurized you, and if there's a diplomatic incident then it's my head, not yours." Sussock leaned forward.

"I don't know, sir. Really . . ." But the drawer was already open.

"I'd like you to stay here," said Sussock, sitting in the chair. "I may need a witness."

"What for?"

"Well, I don't know until I find it. That's the nature of my work, spending a lot of time and energy looking for something without knowing exactly what we're looking for." Sussock was speaking more to himself than to the commissionaire. "You see, if we knew what we were looking for we'd not have to spend so much time looking for it."

"I don't understand."

"Neither do I, my friend," said Sussock wearily. "Neither do I. Just stick around, please."

Bill McGarrigle's desk had three drawers arranged in a tier on the right-hand side. Sussock opened them from bottom to top. The bottom drawer seemed to be the drawer in which Bill McGarrigle had kept his personal possessions, a paperback novel about the war in the desert, a book about walking the Highland Way, and a pair of slippers.

"Bill McGarrigle have difficulty with his feet?" asked Sussock, taking out the slippers and placing them on the floor.

"I don't think so, sir, most reporters keep a pair of casual shoes or slippers for walking about the building, especially the ladies."

Sussock grunted and continued to rummage. There were a couple of copies of *Mayfair* and, in contrast, a well-read copy of the poetry of T. S. Eliot; there was a mug, badly tea-stained, and a handkerchief with "B McG" stitched to the corner, and a copy of the Caledonian MacBrayne summer timetable. Sussock opened the timetable and noticed that the sailings from Wemyss Bay to Rothesay had been underlined in red pen. He replaced the items and tugged open the middle drawer, which revealed itself to be Bill McGarrigle's tool box, a dictionary, a thesaurus, a chipped mug full of ballpoint pens, a copy of the *Guide to Simple English*, a small directory of the phone numbers of other organizations and agencies and a list of people's extension numbers within the *Clarion* building. In the top drawer Sussock found the two articles he had hoped to find, McGarrigle's notebook and diary. His surge of delight was superseded by yet another disappointment in what was, for him, turning out to be a disappointing weekend. Bill McGarrigle used shorthand and so his notebook was meaningless to Sussock. Moreover McGarrigle, who already looked to Sussock to have been a bit of a slob, had entered his appointments in his diary in code. On the day that he received a blow on the back of the head which was to cause

his death some forty-eight hours later, Bill
McGarrigle's diary read:

Wednesday	July 15
4. Mrs. D	
7. SS. c. G. Rmst.	

"One diary and one notebook," said
Sussock. "I'm taking these away with me."

"Very good, sir," said the
commissionaire.

"Could you keep this desk in quarantine,
as it were, chief?"

"Aye, no bother, sir." The
commissionaire tore off a sheet of A4 from
the pad on Bill McGarrigle's desk and,
taking a ballpoint pen, wrote: "Do not
touch. Police investigation in progress—S
Mc."

"Everybody uses codes around here,"
said Sussock.

"Don't you, sir?"

"Aye, but I can understand those. 'S
Mc'—is that you?"

"It is. They call me Super Mac on account
of my name being McMillan."

"Dates you a bit, doesn't it?" Even for Sussock, "Super Mac" was going back into the dark ages.

"It's lost on the younger ones, but names stick, you know."

"I know."

"Anyway this should keep them away, sir. I'll tape it down after you've gone."

At 9.00 a.m. Montgomerie returned to the tenement block in Rutherglen and began checking the twenty-seven flats from which he had received no answer the previous evening. The interviews went pretty much as they had gone on the Friday night, those that did answer their door had all heard about the attack but had either been out on the night in question or had been at home but seen nothing. Montgomerie was already of the impression that his was an assignment of stone-turning rather than investigation, and saw the end of the task as being the point when the last door closed on him. Then he rang the doorbell underneath the name "Laing".

"Yes, I saw him," she said, smiling.

"You saw him!"

"Yes." She was middle-aged, face heavy

with make-up, lacquered hair, pearls, expensive dress.

"Why didn't you contact the police?" Montgomerie was more dumbfounded than angry.

"Why didn't you contact me? I've been waiting for over two days."

"Well, what did you see?"

"I saw him attack the other man, look up because I was tapping on the window to make him stop, then he ran away."

"And you then sat and waited for the police?"

"Yes. Well, I mean I'd done my bit, hadn't I? Rattling the window like I did made him stop, didn't it?"

Montgomerie paused to gain some self-control and then asked what the man looked like.

"Oh, I'm not really that good with words. Couldn't I draw one of those little pictures?"

"You'll have to come to the station for that," said Montgomerie.

"I'll be ready in about an hour. Will you send a car for me?" She smiled again and then shut the door.

Montgomerie went into the backs and kicked a beer can over the wall into the school yard.

At 9.15 a.m. Richard King walked thankfully out of the heat and entered the shade of a cool close in Langside. He took his tie from his jacket pocket and clipped it on to his collar while starting up the stairs to the second floor and a door with a highly polished brass plate embossed with the name "McGarrigle". He tapped on the door.

"Oh, it's you, is it?" From holding the door with her hand, Bill McGarrigle's daughter leant against the door. "I suppose there are more insensitive times to call but I can't think of one right off."

"I'm sorry, love."

"No, you're not. You don't give a damn." She spoke icily through a small mouth, a voice of pent-up anger. "This is just another job to you, just one more old man, another statistic to add to the growth of violence in the streets which keeps people like you in a job. Have you never heard of crime prevention? Where were you when he was being killed, eh? Nowhere to be seen. But you swarm round when it's safe and when it's too late to do anything. Cops!"

"If I could call back another time I would, love . . ."

"And it's Miss McGarrigle to you, not 'love'."

"All right, Miss McGarrigle," said King, trying not to let his own voice harden. "I'm very sorry to have to call at a time such as this but it's important. We haven't exactly got all the time in the world and we want to catch the man who killed your father, but the trail's getting colder by the minute and your anger isn't helping any."

The girl was silent for a moment and then said, "I'm sorry I spoke like that . . ." She let her hand slip from the door and King entered the flat. The curtains were drawn shut and the flat was gloomy and airless with the smell of the kitchen refuse beginning to rise. Two suitcases, still packed and strapped tight with leather belts, stood side by side in the hall.

"She insisted on finishing the packing," explained the young woman. "Last night after the man from the hospital called to tell us and deliver the certificate, she started to pack his case and made it right for his holiday. Then she broke down and insisted we shut all the windows and curtains. I called the doctor and he gave her something. She's still out. The doctor told me to open a window in her room. I think I'll open some others."

"It'll give you something to do," said King.

"It gets like that, doesn't it? Suddenly your life is nothing, you've got nothing to keep you busy. I still think it's a dream and I keep expecting him to come home and put his slippers on and ask me to get him a mug of tea. It's right what they say, isn't it?"

"What's that?"

"That it's not the hole that people fill when they die that's important, it's the hole they leave behind them."

"I think that's true, but you shouldn't feel so guilty about anything you might have done or said over the last few years. I reckon if your dad could have his life over again he would have wanted it just the same."

"You think so?"

"I think so."

"Are you married?" asked the young woman suddenly.

"Yes," said King.

"Children?"

"Two. Both very young."

"That's nice," said the girl. "That sounds so very nice."

"It is." King privately conceded that it was very, very nice, and felt uncomfortable that here, amid grief and frightened adolescence, it was his cup which runneth over. "Miss McGarrigle. . ."

"Call me Emma," she said. "I'm sorry for what I said at the door."

"That's all right."

"What shall I call you?"

"Mr. King," he said firmly. "Emma, when I called here on Thursday you said that your father had a study. Can I see it?"

"Yes, of course." She stood and walked down the hallway. "He's got tons of paper in there, it'll take hours to sort. Would you like a cup of tea?" She stopped and opened a door.

"Yes," said King. "Thanks. That would be great."

Bill McGarrigle's study was a small room. One wall was lined with books, a small roll-top desk stood underneath the window, the third wall was taken up by shelving on which lay boxes filled with papers or with sheets of printed matter lying loosely. The fourth wall was wholly taken up by the doorway. The room was dark and King flung open the curtains and then, remembering himself, shut them again.

"You can have the curtains open if you wish," said Emma McGarrigle, who had appeared silently at the doorway.

"I'll settle for the light," King replied, reaching for the switch. "I'll also open the window a wee bit."

"What are you looking for? Clues?"

"Yes," said King, opening the window.

"Dad used to spend a lot of time in here. Reading, writing letters, mostly reading."

"Didn't your father ever clean it out?"

"Never saw him throwing anything out. He didn't like me and her going in here and he'd never let her dust in here. This was his den, he'd sort of hide in here while me and her were battling it out in the living-room."

She left the study and walked away, reappearing a few moments later with a mug of tea. "Can I help?" she said. "I've always been good at finding things."

"Away you go, hen," replied King.

"But . . ."

"Shut the door behind you, Emma."

She slammed the door shut and marched away down the hallway.

The thousands of sheets of paper and hundreds of books were not as daunting as King had at first thought. He reasoned that if a guy lives in a mess and chucks his possessions all over the shop without rhyme or reason, there develops a certain order in the environment he creates. Any article in day to day use or of current relevancy is located within easy reach or at the top of the pile until it is superseded, whereupon it begins to sink. King sat back in the chair, sipping the tea and trying to get the "feel" of the room, noting where the rough divisions lay and where similar articles were clustered. The pens, for example, enjoyed a definite grouping on the right-hand side of the desk's writing surface, although old pencils and "dead' ballpoints were also littered sporadically around the room. King noticed that a copy of the *Evening Times* dated Tuesday the 14th lay on a shelf to the left of the desk. It was probably the last one Bill McGarrigle had bought, certainly it was the last one he had brought home. He drained the mug and placed it on the floor so as not to let it intrude in the delicate balance of the room, and then reasoned that if anything in the room was relevant to Bill

McGarrigle's murder it would be within easy reach and not buried under papers and books and odd chattels which had taken years to accumulate. He found it under the four-day-old copy of the *Evening Times*. It was a folder in stiff brown cardboard marked clearly at the top corner "Gilheaney". There was just a single sheet of paper in the folder which to King's disappointment didn't seem to contain a great deal to go on:

		Gilheaney
Mrs. D	S	
£	McSW	
£?		
McSW	AM (FFM)?	

King left Bill McGarrigle's study with the folder under his arm and walked into the living-room. Emma McGarrigle was sitting in one of the armchairs, staring vacantly into the gloom, showing no trace of her recent anger or uplift.

"Emma," said King, "I'm taking this file away with me."

The girl didn't say anything, she just turned her head slightly and glanced at King. He turned away and behind him the girl said, "He's not coming back, is he?" King stopped momentarily, but continued to the door and let himself out. As he was getting into his car he noticed that the flats on the opposite side of the street and the flats on the same stair as the McGarrigles' had closed curtains; a community's gesture of sympathy.

12.10 p.m. Donoghue, Sussock, King and Montgomerie sat in a semi-circle in Donoghue's office, in front of the desk behind which sat Chief Superintendent Findlater. The conference began with members reading through photocopies of the pathologist's report, a report from the laboratory of Forensic Scientific Investigation, a sheet containing the abbreviations found in Bill McGarrigle's diary and study, and copies of hastily handwritten reports from Montgomerie, King and Sussock. Richard King balanced a notebook on his lap; being the junior man, he had been designated minute-taker.

"So you're convinced it's not a bar brawl or chance attack," said Findlater in his deep

Highland accent. "These reports indicate the attacker was a bit of a yob?"

"No." Donoghue cleared his throat. "No, sir, I'm not convinced of anything but I do think the whole situation is suspicious." He pressed a twist tobacco into his pipe bowl. "My suspicion is that Bill McGarrigle was hunting down a story, got too close to something and was murdered because of it."

"So point one, what was McGarrigle investigating?" Findlater nodded to King, who scribbled on his notepad. "And why didn't he inform us?"

"His job was at risk," said King. "Like I said in my report, if he didn't start producing he was for the chop. I think he must have been quite desperate, he was a modestly living family man who had suddenly found that his job wasn't his for life."

"So he started out on investigative journalism, hit a rich seam and burrowed away until he was killed." Donoghue lit his pipe with his gold-plated lighter. "If we follow the same enquiry we ought to end up at the same place."

"Without the same result, I hope,"

grunted Findlater, a huge man who even in a sitting position dominated the room.

"Where do we start?" asked Sussock. "Do you think the coded entries in the diary hold a clue?"

"I think they must," said Donoghue, holding up the sheet of paper containing the photocopies of the page of McGarrigle's diary and the sheet found in the folder. "Heaven above knows what it means."

Wednesday	July 15
4. Mrs. D	
7. SS. c. G.	Rmst.
	Gilheaney
Mrs. D	S
£	McSW
£?	
McSW	AM (FFM)?

"I think it's a simple abbreviation," said Montgomerie.

"Simple?" asked Findlater.

"Yes, sir." Montgomerie shifted on his seat. "Take his diary: there seem to be two appointments. One is for a Mrs. D who also crops up later under the heading 'Gilheaney' which we think may be relevant."

"He mentioned that name while still semi-conscious," said Findlater.

"Right, sir. The second appointment, SScG Rmst, I would suggest is a meeting with someone whose initials are SS."

"What then is Rmst?" asked Sussock.

"It stands for Rutherglen Main Street, which is about a hundred yards from where his body was found."

"That makes sense," said Donoghue, nodding. "What do you make of 'c.G'?"

"Well, the letter 'c' is used by historians as an abbreviation for 'circa', about, to indicate, an approximate date or period, such as c. 1066, for example."

"I know that," said Donoghue.

"Well, if we widen the meaning of the word 'about' and say that in this context 'c' denotes, say, 'in respect of ' or 'to do with', so that at seven o'clock on the fifteenth of July Bill McGarrigle was meeting SS about G, Gilheaney."

"He was meeting this SS on Rutherglen Main Street to talk about Gilheaney?" said Findlater.

"I think that's a reasonable assumption,"

Donoghue said, taking his pipe from his mouth. "We certainly have to start with a hypothesis at some stage. What about the rest of it?"

"Well." Montgomerie studied the sheet of paper. "There certainly seems to be a chain of events here, or a system being linked up. It starts with a Mrs. D whom McGarrigle met on the day he died. She appears later as being connected with S. There follows a symbol for money and a question mark. What that means is not clear."

"Whose money is it, what is it for, where has it gone?" said Findlater.

"Yes, sir. That sort of thing." Montgomerie nodded. "The rest is still a bit of a mystery."

"It reduces to three, really," suggested Donoghue. "Who or what is SS, who or what is McSW, and who or what is AM (FFM)?"

"That's one line of enquiry," agreed Findlater clutching the sheet of paper in his huge hands. "What do they all stand for?"

"Yes, I was going to propose that we follow two lines of enquiry," said Donoghue. "We have the forensic and path

66

lab reports here. Bill McGarrigle died from a blow to the head which fractured his skull and led to a massive haemorrhage. The report indicates he was struck from behind, with the fracture to the rear and above the right ear and with a slightly inclined plane."

"Which indicates what?" Findlater raised his eyebrows.

"In itself, sir, nothing, but if we make the assumption, and I know this is a dangerous business, but if we make the assumption that this was the first blow struck, from behind, at a vulnerable part of the body, to disable the victim prior to setting about the ribs and the legs, then we may draw some indications about the physical make-up of the attacker."

"Such as him being a right-hander?" suggested King.

"Yes, I would say so."

Donoghue pulled on his pipe. "I would also suggest we are looking for a small man, otherwise the fracture would have a horizontal plane, or one inclined down towards the front of the head instead of up." Donoghue checked the front sheet of the pathologist's report. "Bill McGarrigle was a man of medium height, five-eight, and so his assailant was probably considerably shorter, but at the same time he was no weakling. The murder weapon is a length of mild steel tube weighing nearly ten pounds. He would have had to carry it around with him for a while before swinging it, because according to Forensic there's no indication it was a bit of metal which was lying in the back court rusting away which was picked up by chance."

"No fingerprints either," Findlater looked at the report from the Forensic lab. "Just Bill McGarrigle's hair and blood, and a circumference which is conducive to the injury sustained."

"Oh, it's the murder weapon all right," said Donoghue. "The cleanliness aspect is important: it implies premeditation. It adds weight to the theory that the attack was in connection with whatever Bill McGarrigle was working on."

"You were talking about the attacker, sir." King's pen was poised over his notebook.

"Yes, thank you." Donoghue cleared his throat. "It's a length of metal which was carried for an indefinite amount of time, wielded with some considerable force for three or four blows, then carried for the hundred-yards-plus run to the railway bridge and thrown on to the tracks. How far from the bridge did you find it, Montgomerie?"

"Twenty, twenty-five feet, sir."

"So it was thrown some considerable distance?"

"Yes, sir."

"Even allowing for the adrenalin pumping through his body that's quite a bit of physical endurance. I believe he's small and strong and a right-hander."

"It isn't much to go on." Findlater leafed through the reports which were spread in front of him.

The telephone on Donoghue's desk rang.

"It's all we have," replied Donoghue, ignoring the telephone. "And even then I'm the first to admit that it's based on the twin assumption that he acted alone and the blow to Bill McGarrigle's skull was the first blow of the attack."

"What do you propose, Inspector?"

"Well, sir, I'd like Montgomerie to follow the murder enquiry." Donoghue glanced at his telephone with annoyance. "I'd like Detective-Sergeant Sussock and

Detective-Constable King to follow up on whatever Bill McGarrigle was working on. The two investigations should converge at some point." He stood, walked to his desk and snatched the telephone. "Look, whoever you are, if I've said it once, I've said it a thousand times, if I haven't answered my phone by the second ring I'm either out or engaged, and right now I'm . . ." He paused, his grip on the telephone relaxing. "All right, someone will be right down." He replaced the telephone. "That was Constable Piper on the front desk. He has a lady with him, a Mrs. Dinn. She has just seen the first edition of the *Evening Times* and would like to know who is going to see about her money now that Mr. McGarrigle is dead?"

4

KING had noticed that it was not an unusual occurrence, not a strange way to crack a case. They'd come face to face with a brick wall and had no way to turn when someone would phone in or amble up to the desk sergeant and say, "Excuse me, I'm sorry to bother you, but I thought you might like to know . . ." He looked at the man, then the woman and then looked again at the man. He said he didn't understand.

"It's so simple," said the man and then said something to the woman, who snorted and said something to the man, who replied vociferously.

"Hang about." King held up his hand and the chatter stopped.

"Mrs. Dinn is very angry, sir," said the man.

"I can see that." King glanced at his notes. "But I'm not going to be able to help unless you can make me understand."

The man spoke to the woman, who replied sharply.

"Mrs. Dinn thinks you are very stupid, sir," said the man.

King dragged a slow smile across his face.

"She says she will not tell you again, sir."

"She's going to have to."

"She's a very stubborn lady, sir."

"I'm beginning to see that." King looked at the woman. "Tell Mrs. Dinn that this is a murder enquiry and if she doesn't co-operate I'll arrest her for obstructing the police by withholding information."

"She will not like that, sir," said the man apologetically.

"Just tell her."

The man spoke to the woman, who then glared at King and began to shout at him. She was dressed in a brilliantly coloured sari, with a gold pin fastened to the side of her nose. She had a small face and a hooked nose, and she sat there, fixing him with dark eyes, shooting words at him.

"Mrs. Dinn is saying that freely she came and freely she will depart, sir," explained the man with the turban. He had a lean and open look, with a neatly trimmed, greying beard. King put his age as about sixty, some twenty years older, he thought, than Mrs. Dinn.

King cleared his throat and managed to stop Mrs. Dinn in full flow. "Do you understand Mrs. Dinn's complaint, Mr. Bano?"

"Perfectly, sir."

King had initially recoiled from the smell of Mrs. Dinn and Mr. Bano, but rapidly detected and began to enjoy the scent which lay behind the smell. He was also recognizing Mr. Bano to be one of the most well-mannered men he had ever met while undertaking his duties.

"Perhaps, Mr. Bano," said King, "if I tell you what I think to be the situation you could correct me if I go wrong?"

"Delighted, sir."

"Well," said King, consulting his notebook, "Mrs. Dinn here and her husband sold their grocer's shop some five years ago."

"Five years, seven months on the twenty-eighth day of this month, sir."

"Right. So the person who bought the shop paid the money to Mrs. Dinn's solicitors."

"No, sir."

"No?"

"No. The gentleman who purchased the shop and was a cousin of Mrs. Dinn's paid the money to his solicitors."

"I see. And the solicitor engaged by the purchaser then paid the money to the solicitor acting for Mrs. Dinn, the vendor."

"That is correct, sir. Five years and seven months ago."

"But Mrs. Dinn's solicitors have not released the money to Mrs. Dinn?"

"That is correct."

"She alleges they have kept it?"

"They have kept it. We have written letters and telephoned and it has been promised us, in the next few months we are going to get it. For the last five years we expect to receive it in the next few months."

"Can I ask how much money is involved?"

"Thirty-five thousand pounds. Five years ago thirty-five thousand pounds was a lot of money, enough to buy the house we wanted. If we are paid in full tomorrow we could not now buy half of the house."

"That's inflation," said King wearily.

"So it is also stealing money."

"Only in an abstract sense." King tapped

his pen on the desk. "I—er—I'm not sure that the police can be of help, Mr. Bano."

"But who can help us?"

"I'm not sure. I'll have to get advice but in itself this seems to me to be a civil law issue, not a criminal act. Perhaps you ought to take legal advice, take out an injunction against your solicitors."

"We have taken legal advice, sir. It has cost us thirty-five thousand pounds."

"I appreciate your anger, Mr. Bano, but I'm just explaining the police point of view." King chewed the end of his pen. "If you can substantiate an allegation of fraud or some other criminal act we might be able to take a look at this firm, but even then there's no guarantee that you'd get your money back."

"Oh my," said Mr. Bano and looked up at the naked light-bulb.

"Who are they anyway?"

"They have a small office in Byres Road, above a butcher's shop. They are called McNulty, Spicer and Watson."

"McSW," said King.

"I'm sorry, sir?"

"Oh nothing." King shook his head.

"Which of these gentlemen are you dealing with?"

"Mr. Spicer. We are clients of Mr. Spicer."

"And you approached Mr. McGarrigle and asked him to help."

"No, sir. He approached us a few weeks ago and he showed us a letter we had written to the *Clarion* newspaper nearly one year ago."

"No, I think his hair was longer."

Stan Greene peeled away a sheet of polythene and replaced it with another.

"That's about right," said Mrs. Laing nodding with approval. "I reckon that's about it."

"What, the whole thing?" Stan Greene looked at her. Montgomerie walked from the wall where he had been standing, and leaned over the table, looking at the photofit. "That's him?" he asked.

"That's his hair, Officer." Mrs. Laing sat back in the chair with her hands folded on her lap. "Only his hair. Now we're going to do the rest of him. He had a nice nose, a bit on the large side but nice, you know, clean lines."

"Clean lines," sighed Stan Greene and searched through sheets of polythene. Montgomerie sank back against the wall.

It had taken Mrs. Laing one hour and forty-five minutes to get the hair constructed to her satisfaction. It now also seemed that she had an exact impression of his face, and all this from a glimpse of the man in the gloom and from thirty feet above.

"His cheeks were a bit fuller," she said.

Montgomerie leaned forward and took a second look. The photofit was still minus mouth and chin but the man whom Mrs. Laing saw murder Bill McGarrigle was already looking to be a staggeringly handsome individual. Two and a half hours after she had started she relaxed in the chair and looked up at Montgomerie with a didn't-I-do well expression. "That's him," she said.

"Not unlike Tyrone Power, is he?" said Montgomerie drily, looking at the completed photofit, and not any Quasimodo himself.

"That's him, Officer. That's the one."

Montgomerie escorted her to the main entrance of the police station and thanked her for her time. Three hours to go through the mug shots and turn up nothing and a further two and a half hours to create an image of her fantasy. He watched her force a straight path through the holiday crowds, head held high and her huge rear waddling in the thin cotton dress.

In the CID room he wrote up Mrs. Laing's visit in the McGarrigle file. Stan Greene approached him and handed him a wad of photocopies of the photofit. Montgomerie apologized for wasting his time.

"Don't know how she's got the brass neck," said Greene.

"We might succeed in getting the interest of the film companies if nothing else," smiled Montgomerie. "Split the agent's fee fifty-fifty. It'll pay better than public service. Coffee?"

"I could use one right enough, Mal, but I'd better go. I promised to take the family to Saltcoats for the Fair weekend. We're only seven hours late getting away."

"Your professionalism is an example to us all."

"The hell with professionalism, I need the money. I've got a thing called a mortgage and a wife who believes that her place is in the home even though the kids are old enough to allow her to get a job."

"Still, thanks for coming in, Stan. I wish I could say it was worth it."

Montgomerie filed the photocopies except one, signed out and drove to Rutherglen. He climbed a dark stairway, the air of which had grown musty with the heat and rapped on the door of Timofei Jaruduski. He rapped twice more before he received an answer.

"Who is?" yelled a voice from the other side of the door.

"Police," said Montgomerie. "I called the other day, remember?"

"About the sighting?"

"Aye."

"I told you everything. Is not good. Go now." Montgomerie could tell by the strength of the voice that Jaruduski had come towards the door and was now standing directly behind it.

"There's something I'd like you to look at, Mr. Jaruduski."

"Go. What is it?"

"A photograph."

"What of a photograph?"

"Probably of the man who attacked the newspaper man in your back court."

"Was not a man who did it?"

"Will you look at the photograph?"

"Wait."

Montgomerie waited and then a clove of garlic dropped out of the letter-box and landed at his feet. He picked it up.

"Move away," yelled Jaruduski. "Back to the door of the kind lady."

Montgomerie retreated across the flagstones until he stood against the further door. Jaruduski's letter-box opened.

"I have to see," he said. "Put the photograph on the floor."

"Mr. Jaru—"

"It must be so. Please, on the floor."

Montgomerie laid the photocopy down.

"Now you must break the garlic and smear it over the photograph. Both sides."

Montgomerie broke open the clove of garlic and kneeled on the dusty flagstones, drawing the vegetable across both sides of the paper.

"Now bring here."

Montgomerie folded the paper and passed it through the letter-box.

Jaruduski snatched it and the letter-box

80

lid snapped shut. Moments later it was opened and the piece of paper was pushed out. "Now go," said Jaruduski.

Montgomerie unfolded the paper. Across the front, right over the clean-cut features, in block letters, Jaruduski had printed "I see only wings." Montgomerie went down into the street, he felt it was useless to take it any further. He went back to the station, wrote up the visit to Jaruduski, which took him fifteen seconds and then signed himself out until 6.30 p.m. It was Fair Saturday, 4.00 p.m.

He knew he'd be working that evening, hoofing around the bars and the streets of Rutherglen, showing the photofit to publicans, bus drivers and taxi drivers. Montgomerie had wide shoulders, a slim waist, a downturned moustache, and for the last nine years, since he was seventeen, he had had his pick of women. So much so that he had lost count of the number, though none of them could have been called a conquest, all finding his good looks and charm utterly irresistible. Having briefly explored one, he would await the next, and the next. Then he met Fiona.

Fiona was different.

He could not leave Fiona. She was charming and intelligent and mature and went in and out in all the right places. She also had the rare and priceless virtue of enabling Montgomerie to retain a sense of independence and freedom in their relationship. At 4.00 p.m. on Fair Saturday he took time out to visit Fiona.

He had known Fiona for two years, meeting over a pile of blood-soaked clothing and a recent stiff. She was the casualty doctor, he was the cop that had brought in the raw material. She was a career woman and made few demands on him, which suited Montgomerie down to the ground. But recently he had found himself spending more and more time in her flat. As a man who had always loved his freedom, he found this unsettling.

He let himself into her flat. She was sitting under the window on a scatter cushion reading the *Glasgow Herald*. She held up her hand palm outwards as Montgomerie entered the room and then let it fall to grasp the mug of coffee which lay on the varnished floorboards. She didn't take her eyes off the newspaper. He went back into the hallway and tugged off his boots and padded back into the main room in his stocking feet.

"Malcolm!" Fiona put her newspaper down. "How nice to see you!" She smiled and held out her hand. Montgomerie took it and kissed her forehead. "I thought you were working all day. You know, the Edinbrovian slave-driver cracking his whip."

"Did I say that?" Montgomerie peeled off his jacket and slung it on one of the scatter cushions.

Fiona read her newspaper.

"When did I say that?" He sat next to her and slid his arm around her waist.

Fiona turned the page. Montgomerie got up, grabbed his jacket and hung it in the hall.

"Last night," she said, smiling as he entered the room.

"I don't remember." He resumed his seat next to her. "But it's true right enough, we have a murder investigation, happened just before the Fair and Fabian cancelled all leave. Ray Sussock's fuming. He had a weekend planned in his love-nest near Mallaig with the delectable WPC Willems.

She's gone off by herself and left him in Big G."

"Do they think their affair is a secret?" Fiona laughed.

"They're convinced of it, they make a big show of avoiding each other in public but everybody knows what's happening."

"Oh yes, and what exactly is happening?"

"The same thing that I have planned for us two." He kissed her.

"Suppose I said I was going out, this very minute, as a matter of fact?"

"I would say that's not true." He slid his hand inside her T-shirt. "I do remember something being said last night, something about you drawing Fair Saturday night in casualty with them coming in bleeding from every orifice. So you don't have to be there until six, which gives you plenty of time to allow me to consult you about this pain I have, Doctor."

Fiona's body was firm and smooth. She put everything into the act, and moaned until she screamed. Afterwards they lay there, with the sun streaming through the halfopen curtains, talking quietly.

King tapped reverently at the door. Emma

McGarrigle opened it. "She's still in her room," she said. "She hasn't come out and won't take anything to eat."

"Give her time," said King. "I'd like to have another look inside your dad's study, please."

Emma McGarrigle stepped aside and beckoned him in the house. He walked to Bill McGarrigle's study and sat in the chair.

"Would you like a cup of tea again, Mr. King?" asked the girl from the doorway.

"No, thank you, love." King didn't turn as he spoke. "Turn the light on for me, please, and shut the door. I'll see you before I leave."

King sat in Bill McGarrigle's chair for a few moments looking at his surroundings, the mounds of papers and books, piled on the floor and spilling off the shelves, trying again to get the "feel" of the study. Presently he got up from the chair and began to probe the shelves and the drawers as carefully as he could so as not to disturb the order of the papers. Near to where he had found the folder which had been labelled "Gilheaney", and a few inches deeper in the pile, he came across a long, brown envelope. It was unmarked but King had long felt that

Bill McGarrigle had been a man who had no need of labels and a filing system. King sensed that even the name "Gilheaney" written on the folder had been done only in the spirit of thoughtless doodling, rather than in an attempt at filing efficiently.

In the envelope were photocopies of two letters of complaint sent to the editor of the *Clarion*. Both letters alleged loss of monies to the law firm of McNulty, Spicer and Watson. There was a period of nearly twelve months separating the dates of the letters, the second having been written less than six weeks previously. King resumed his seat. He imagined the *Clarion* receiving hundreds, thousands of letters each year complaining of poor service, crime, unfair treatment. Some were probably followed up, others, the vast majority, were probably dismissed as malicious or petty or as having no foundation. But it seemed that all the letters had been kept, for a year at least. King could visualize Bill McGarrigle, in a cold sweat about losing his job, searching the old letters looking for a story. And he'd found one; hell, had he found one.

The second of the two letters had been written by a man who had given his name as Eric Simpson and whose address was in Queens Cross. King drove there.

Most of Queens Cross had come down and much of the rest was coming down, with a couple of blocks of the old sandstones being gutted by a Housing Association prior to being refurbished. The dust from the demolition sites hung in the still summer air and never seemed to fall completely to the ground. There were forty or fifty flats still inhabited in an old tenement block which stood between two demolition sites. Eric Simpson lived in one of the flats.

King climbed the stairway, reading the name on each door as he passed it. It wasn't until he got to the very top that he saw "Simpson" written on a piece of paper which was taped to the door.

"The smooth stinking swine," said Simpson after King had introduced himself and explained the purpose of his visit.

"Shall we talk here or inside?" asked King.

Simpson stepped aside and shut the door behind King. His flat was a single end: one room off a common stairway. His bed was hard against one wall, there was a table in the middle of the floor and a couple of easy chairs in the bay window, and there was a wash-hand-basin in a recess.

"So you're on to him at last," said Simpson, pushing his shirt into his jeans. He had wild ginger hair and a face like a pile of broken glass; he had a nearly toothless mouth and a dazed expression. The scars on his face extended down his neck. King thought he was about twenty-five.

"On to who?"

"Spicer. The wee rat." Simpson went over to the cooker and lighted the ring under the kettle. He went back across the room and sank on to the bed and held his head in his hands.

"Bevvied?" asked King.

"Aye." He reached under the bed and pulled out a cardboard box. It was half full of cans of lager and bottles of wine. "I've been having a wee drink since Thursday," he explained in a voice like pit boots on gravel. "I got laid off on Thursday."

"Redundant?"

"Aye. Me and twenty-five others. What's today, sir?"

"Saturday. Call me Mr. King, please."

"Saturday?" Simpson ran his hands

through his hair and then bent forward and picked up a half-smoked roll-up from the floor. "Saturday, aye, it's Fair Saturday, is it no?"

"Aye," said King.

"Aye," sighed Simpson and struck a match clumsily. He held it unsteadily while he lit the dog-end, holding the flame to the tobacco much longer than necessary. "Will you take a wee heavy, Mr. King?"

"No, thanks," said King.

The man's eyes hardened. He took the roll-up from his mouth and stared at King. Dangerous game, refusing drinks from Glaswegians.

"Can't," said King. "I'm on duty."

"You can't?"

King shook his head. "I'd get my books."

Simpson grunted and took a deep drag on the roll-up. "I got my books on Thursday," he said. "I've been having a wee drink since then."

"Aye," said King.

The kettle began to whistle. Simpson walked unsteadily across the room and brought it over to the table. He dropped a tea bag into the least dirty cup, slopped some hot water into it, shovelled some powdered milk in and gave the brew half a stir with the handle of a fork. No, thought King, please don't, please don't ask if . . .

"Will you take a cup of tea, Mr. King?"

"Aye," said King. "That would be fine."

Simpson created a similar mess of tea for King and handed it to him in a waxy cup.

"Thanks," said King. "Live alone?"

"The wife's away to her ma's. We had a wee row and I gave her a wee doin'."

"Not been your week, has it?" He lifted the cup to his mouth, balked at the next step and lowered it slowly to the table.

"Och, she'll be back."

"Reckon?"

"Aye. She's always away to her ma's."

"Knock her about a lot, do you?"

"You know how it is."

King knew how it was and he knew Simpson was probably right. She'd be back in a few days and put up with a hell of a lot because she'd grown up with it and didn't know any different. But right then it wasn't his concern.

"What happened between you and Spicer?"

"Him, Spicer. I'll tell you what happened between me and wee Spicer." He sat on the bed, jabbing the air with the hand which held the dog-end, then said, "Och aye," and his head sagged forward. King waited. Moments later Simpson slowly raised his head and looked at King. "Listen, it was a while ago, I was in another world, on another Planet. I had good money coming in and me and her were getting on. We had a bit put by and we thought we'd get a wee house. We saw one in Dennistoun, two rooms, a kitchen and an inside lavatory. We went to the council for a loan and they said we needed a solicitor and so we got on to Mr. Spicer. Spicer the wee rat. We opened an account with him and gave him our money."

"How much?"

"Three thousand five hundred pounds," said Simpson and then repeated the sum slowly, more to himself than to King.

"So what happened?"

"We kept getting loans from the council so we could put in bids for houses and Spicer kept cancelling the loans when our bids weren't taken."

"How long did this go on?"

"Year, year and a bit."

"So then?"

"So then we asked Mr. Spicer for our money back and you know how much we had left? We had five hundred and forty-three pounds. I remember the amount because it's in reverse order, five-four-three, like that."

King breathed deeply. "What was his story?"

"He said it had gone on looking over our houses, I mean—" Simpson made a circular motion with his hand—"the houses we put in bids for."

"Surveyor's fees?"

"Aye, that's what he said." Simpson pulled on the dog-end but it was done and the tip burnt his finger. He threw it on the floor and stamped on it.

"Did you see the surveys?"

"No. You never do. We only saw the bills. He showed us the bills."

"Do you remember the name of the surveyor?"

"I've got a bill somewhere." Simpson pulled himself off the bed and walked shakily across the floor to the window, leaned under a chair and pulled out a biscuit tin. He rummaged among the contents of the tin and then held up a piece of paper, looking at King. King walked over and took the piece of paper. It was headed "Shawlands Surveyors—Domestic and Commercial Properties".

"Can I keep this?" asked King.

"Aye. It's nae use to me."

"We'll likely be back to take a statement, Mr. Simpson."

"Just let me know when you hang the bastard." Simpson sank into the chair and closed his eyes.

On his way back to the city centre King stopped at a telephone kiosk and checked the yellow pages. There was no listing for "Shawlands Surveyors".

It was 6.00 p.m., Fair Saturday.

6.30 p.m. Fair Saturday. King and Sussock sat in Donoghue's office. Donoghue took his pipe from his mouth and raised his coffee to his lips. He sipped and then asked, "Are we getting anywhere, gentlemen? Is there progress?"

"I think so, sir," said King. "The focus seems to be shifting. Gilheaney's probably just another guy who got ripped off by Spicer."

"If anybody got ripped off," said Sussock.

"That's right," nodded Donoghue. "We have no proof."

"Still," King persisted, "it seems that Bill McGarrigle was chasing Spicer as something rotten in the legal community."

"Looks like it." Donoghue replaced his cup on his desk. "Moves, gentlemen?"

"Do we have any progress from Montgomerie?" asked Sussock.

"None, Ray," said Donoghue, filling his pipe with a blend made up by a city tobacconist to Donoghue's specification. Dutch base with a twist of dark shag for depth of flavour and a slower burning rate. "He's got a fairly fanciful-looking photofit." He held up a copy for King's and Sussock's edification. They both smiled. "He's following it up but his feelings about the witness are such that he's not too hopeful."

"So nothing yet," said Sussock.

"If ever," replied Donoghue, and flicked his lighter and began to draw on his pipe.

"We've nothing to suggest what AM brackets FFM may stand for?" asked King.

"Do you think it's relevant, King?" Donoghue leaned back in his chair. "You said earlier that you thought Spicer was the subject."

"Yes, sir." King edged forward on his chair. "But the order of Bill McGarrigle's abbreviations suggests that Spicer leads on to AM and FFM. Bill McGarrigle probably saw his goal as being beyond Spicer."

"What in the hell was he working on?" Sussock appealed to the others.

"I think I agree with you, King," said Donoghue, pulling and blowing on his pipe, "but it seems that this fellow Spicer is a key unit, a sort of linchpin. He can't be overlooked. Moves, gentlemen?"

"Interview Spicer," said Sussock. "Put some pressure on him. Lean on him."

"Bit drastic, isn't it?" Donoghue raised his eyebrows. "Let's sniff around the man first, he's not going anywhere."

"Go to the senior partner," suggested King.

"That would be my inclination," agreed Donoghue. "Anybody had any dealings with McNulty, Spicer and Watson?"

King and Sussock shook their heads.

"He'll probably be on our list," said King.

"Probably," grunted Donoghue. "The

really successful and senior ones get beyond being called out at 2.00 a.m. to advise suspects." He opened a drawer of his desk and pulled out a booklet of A4 paper and began to run his finger down the columns. "McNab, McNally, McNulty, Abrahams, here we are, McNulty, Spicer and Watson, Office number, home number . . . So what now?"

"Don't beat about the bush," said King. "Telephone him at home."

"And say what?"

"Well . . ."

"Well, King?"

"Well, that enquiries have linked a partner in his firm to a murder. We would like to discuss it with him and . . ."

"And?"

"Well, and to look at the accounts relevant to Spicer's practice."

"What will he say, do you think?"

"He'll tell us to take a running jump."

"Do you think you can persuade him otherwise?"

"Me, sir?"

"You, sir." Donoghue picked up the telephone on his desk, dialled 9 for an outside line and then held it out for King to grasp. King took the telephone and dialled McNulty's home number. A few minutes later he replaced the receiver and said, "He'll be expecting us, sir. This is his address."

5

RORY McNulty's house was a solid stone building, all squares and angles, with a turret room sticking out of the top right-hand side. The house stood between the road and the river at the end of a long driveway which wound round a stand of Scots pine, so that the house could not be seen from the road. Donoghue halted his Rover beside a Rolls-Royce and he and King walked up the steps to the door.

Donoghue rang the bell and then stepped backwards.

The door was opened by a young woman in a black dress. She had a dark complexion and didn't seem to be too worried by the heat. Italian, guessed Donoghue, or possibly Greek, and memories of a holiday came flooding back, his wife tanning in a red bikini, his children kicking at the waves.

"Police," said Donoghue. "Inspector Donoghue and Detective-Constable King to see Mr. McNulty. I believe he's expecting us."

"Please come in," said the girl, stepping aside.

The inside of the house was cool and smelled richly of wood polish and furniture wax. There was a rug on the parquet floor and a tapestry hung on the wall. The girl showed Donoghue and King to a room on the right of the hallway and at the foot of a broad stairway.

"I'll tell Mr. McNulty you're here, gentlemen." The girl spoke in heavily accented but grammatically faultless English. She also impressed Donoghue as being very much at home in the house, very confident, her manner seemed more that of a daughter than a servant or an au pair. She shut the door behind her with a gentle click.

The room was unostentatiously decorated in dark shades with the McNultys' tastes running to woven carpets and solid, expensive furniture. The view from the window looked out over the vale to the distant rooftops of the Bridge of Weir. A large fly buzzed and battered itself against the window, and though neither man spoke they both found the insect a curiously welcome addition. It made the room seem lived in, the house alive.

Donoghue leafed through an atlas which was lying on an occasional table. King walked round the room looking at the prints hanging on the wall. Twenty minutes after they had been shown into the room the door opened. A tall golden-haired man entered. He was wearing cavalry twill slacks, sandals, a silk shirt and a maroon cravat in paisley.

"I'm McNulty," he said.

"Inspector Donoghue." Donoghue and McNulty approached each other and shook hands. Donoghue introduced King.

"Please take a seat." McNulty waved a hand indicating the room. Donoghue sat in a chair, King at the end of a long settee. "What will you drink now? And don't give me any nonsense about being on duty."

"Brandy sour," said Donoghue. "Thank you."

"I think I'd like a lager, sir," said King. "Thank you."

"I think I'll join you in that." McNulty pulled a cord which hung on the wall.

The maid entered the room and McNulty asked her to bring the drinks, addressing her as "Lennie". Short for Leonora, guessed Donoghue, wondering whether it was too late to change his request and also have a lager. He decided against it: he didn't want to appear indecisive.

"Lovely weather," said McNulty, sitting in the chair opposite Donoghue. "Are you going away for the holiday?"

"No, sir," Donoghue replied. "I like to take my main break in September. It's my favourite month. My wife and children are taking a short break, though."

"Yes, I'm fond of September too," said McNulty. "Beautiful evenings. And you, Mr. King, are you going away?"

"No, sir." King shifted his position slightly. "I'll be taking leave, of course, but I'm planning to use it to work on the house."

Lennie brought the drinks into the room, and offered the tray first to Donoghue, then King, and finally McNulty. When she had gone McNulty said. "Well, what is all this?"

"In the course of a murder enquiry, sir," said Donoghue, "our enquiries led to a partner in your firm, a Mr. Spicer."

"John Spicer." McNulty nodded. "Is he under suspicion?"

"No, sir. But our enquiries have revealed that he may have been party to some underhand dealings. In a word, fraud."

"I see." McNulty sipped his lager. "Do

you suspect the whole firm or just John Spicer?"

"Just Mr. Spicer, for the moment."

"For the moment?"

"Yes, sir. For the moment."

"I see. Can I enquire as to the nature of this fraudulent activity?" McNulty rested his glass on the low table.

"Misappropriation of clients' money, withholding clients' money without reason."

"The latter is not a matter for the police, Inspector. Neither is the former unless there has been a complaint. Has there been a complaint? You indicated that you stumbled across these allegations in the course of a murder enquiry."

"There has not been a complaint to us with regard to the misappropriation of client's money," admitted Donoghue, "Only about the withholding of money."

"Which is a matter for the Law Society of Scotland, or else a civil action raised by the client in question." McNulty pyramided his fingers and rested them against his chin. "I fail to see how I can help you, gentlemen."

"There are strong indications that your

firm, particularly Mr. Spicer, is linked to the murder of a journalist who was investigating on behalf of a client who alleges very poor service from Mr. Spicer. We intend to interview Mr. Spicer, but prior to that we'd like to have access to the accounts relevant to Mr. Spicer's work."

"Out of the question. Totally out of the question. There's the matter of professional etiquette. I can't even look at Mr. Spicer's accounts or files, let alone give someone else permission to do so, even if they are police officers. Which reminds me, I haven't seen your identification." Donoghue and King reached into their jackets and McNulty said, "All right, I know a police officer when I see one. Even so, there's also the question of confidentiality."

"The alternative is for us to seize them following a complaint being made," said Donoghue.

"But there has been no complaint."

"This afternoon," said King, "I visited a client of Mr. Spicer. He did not make a complaint as such but he would do if I invited him to. I could note his complaint and take his statement within an hour. We would then get a warrant . . ."

"I know, I know." McNulty sighed. "You need not tell me that it's in my interest to keep this out of the public eye if possible. That firm is my life. What is it you want?"

"We'd like to look at the accounts relevant to Mr. Spicer's practice."

"They're at the outpost."

"The outpost?"

"That's what our sub office has come to be called. It's in Byres Road. We're trying to break into the West End market. Mr. Spicer is in charge there. He has a staff of four, two clerks and two secretaries."

"Do you have keys for the Byres Road office?" asked Donoghue.

"Yes."

"Would you like to accompany us there?"

"When?"

"Now."

"Now! Out of the question, man. I have a social engagement."

"This is a murder enquiry, Mr. McNulty."

"Even so."

"The trail is still hot, as it were," said Donoghue. "We're quite prepared to have a warrant sworn on the basis of the complaint DC King made reference to."

McNulty sat back in the chair. "You don't give me much option," he said. He stood and pulled the cord.

"How long has Mr. Spicer been associated with your firm, sir?" asked Donoghue.

"Since he left school. He joined us as an office boy and then started serving articles. He was taken in as a partner when he was in his early thirties. That was just over ten years ago."

"So now he's in his mid forties?"

"He's forty-three," said McNulty. "He lives with his wife on the Isle of Bute. His wife is much younger than he, still in her twenties, I understand. But they seem happy enough. I dare say that that is all that matters."

Lennie pushed open the door and stood at the entrance to the room, deferentially looking at McNulty.

"Bring me my safari jacket, please, Lennie," said McNulty, "and when Mrs. McNulty returns will you say that I suggest she proceeds to the Baxters' alone. Say that I'll be along later and if she wants to contact me I'll be at the Byres Road office."

"Very good, sir," said Lennie and backed

out of the room, pulling the door shut behind her. She returned a few moments later with McNulty's jacket, still on its hanger.

The three men drove into the city, McNulty following behind in his Rolls-Royce.

It was Fair Saturday, 8.00 p.m.

Sussock pulled the unmarked police car to a stop against the kerb outside a small house in Rutherglen. The heat of the day had subsided and the city was enjoying a pleasantly warm evening. He walked up the drive and went to the back door of the house and rapped on the frame. The door was opened by a young man dressed in a black, tight-fitting T-shirt, baggy trousers and plimsolls. He had a ring in his ear.

"Hello, Daddy," said the young man, smiling. He stood aside as Sussock entered the house. "Meet Benjamin, Daddy."

"Hello," said the other young man who sat on the settee. He wore tight-fitting jeans and clasped his hands together on his lap.

"Mummy's in her room, Daddy," said the first young man and added, by way of

106

explanation, "She saw you coming. She's frightfully upset."

He had recently separated from his wife and the separation had come as a final blissful release. He didn't know where it had gone wrong, probably when their child was born and his wife's disappointment that it was not a girl had not waned, but had developed into entrenched resentment. His wife had become aggressive and openly hostile, their son became homosexual, they colluded against him. When he was reduced to sneaking apologetically in and out of his house and sleeping on the sofa, he decided to quit and took his bedsitter. It was a decision which had brought new hardships but it was a decision which he did not regret.

Sussock went upstairs and into a small room where his remaining belongings had been dumped. He sifted through the cardboard boxes, pulling out some light summer clothes. He went back downstairs and out of the house. As he was walking down the drive his wife flung open an upstairs window. She was a small woman with hurried movements and a pinched face which darted from side to side when she shouted. "And don't come back, I don't want you back here again, just interested in catching robbers, you were never good to me and Samuel."

Sussock drove back to his flat in the West End. He told himself it was all working out, soon the divorce would be through, the house would go up for sale, they'd pay off the building society and split the remainder. Then he'd be solvent. Again. Have enough to put down on a place of his own, a little place like Elka's in Langside. He felt he needed the security of his own bricks and mortar.

Montgomerie dropped Fiona off outside the Glasgow Royal Infirmary and then drove on up to Rutherglen. He parked his car on Rutherglen Main Street and started hoofing round the bars, showing the photofit to the publicans, each time getting the predictable headshaking response. He tried the bus crews, kids in the street, the loners just walking around. It became so routine holding the card up, the headshake and apology, the thanks, that Montgomerie didn't immediately latch on when someone gave him the name and address of a murderer.

It was 9.30 p.m., the evening was still warm but beginning to get dark, though not dark enough for the cars to have to use their headlights. Montgomerie was standing by a telephone kiosk and was in two minds whether to stop an old guy shuffling towards him. The old guy didn't look too observant, his head hung down and he tapped his stick rapidly as he walked. Montgomerie had had a long day, he reckoned he was on a hiding to nothing, just one more, he thought, just one more and then I'm away home, and the last one may as well be the old guy.

"Excuse me, sir," said Montgomerie, and the old man stopped shuffling. He looked up at Montgomerie. "I wonder if I can ask you to look at this picture." He showed the man the photofit. The man took the card and held it in the hand which also held his walking stick.

"Aye," said the man.

"Do you recognize the man, sir?" Montgomerie asked mechanically, already reaching to retrieve the photofit.

"Maybe," said the man.

Montgomerie was pulling the card out of the man's hand before his reply had registered. Then he let it go like it had stung him. "What?"

"This one," said the man, "would he wear a cloak or a cape now?"

"A cape," Montgomerie spluttered. "He probably wears a cape."

"Well, if he does it's him all right."

"Who?"

"Him, sure it is."

"Who is him, sir?"

"Bernie McCusker."

Montgomerie scribbled furiously in his notebook. "Would you know his address, sir?"

"Aye, son. He stays up the stair from me. Fancy wee toff."

"Where's that?"

"Two-two-four Carrick Road. Just around the corner, son."

Montgomerie went back to his car and radioed for assistance. He drove to Carrick Road, parked his car a few closes up from 224 and waited. A few minutes later a Sherpa van with three constables pulled up behind him. Men and women talking in groups turned and looked at the van. Children were grabbed and pulled inside off the street. As soon as the Sherpa pulled up Montgomerie left his car and spoke to the constables in the van. They walked to close number 224. Montgomerie and Piper ran up the stair, one constable stayed at the bottom of the stair and one went into the backs.

The door with "McCusker" on the front was two up on the right. Montgomerie pressed the bell. He heard a scuffling sound inside the flat and pressed the bell again, this time following it up by hammering on the door and yelling "Police!"

Then he heard a shout from outside, looked out of the stair window and saw a figure swing down a rope and kick the constable in the face. The constable went down, the figure fell on him and kicked him in the head a couple of times to make sure he stayed horizontal. Then the figure ran off across the backs with the second constable in hot pursuit.

Montgomerie and Piper ran down the stair and into the backs. Montgomerie ran after the second constable while Piper stopped briefly by the injured man, took off his tunic and slipped it under the man's head, radioed for an ambulance and assistance and then sprinted after

Montgomerie. He ran across the backs, scaling two walls before he finally caught up with the action.

McCusker had his back to a wall which was too high for him to climb. He had grabbed a length of metal which he held in his hands, holding it high over his shoulder like a baseball bat. Montgomerie and the other constable stood just outside swinging distance. When Piper joined the party he took up the left-hand position, only seeing too late that if McCusker did start to swing, he'd be the first one to catch it.

"C'mon, Polis bastards," hissed McCusker. "I'll get one of you."

They didn't need to be told that. This was the end of the line for Bernie McCusker. The problem was how to get in there without copping at least one fractured skull.

Montgomerie didn't know how to work it but he did find time to reflect on the accuracy of Mrs. Laing's photofit. She'd missed the mole on his cheek but other than that, there it was, in the flesh, length of hair, the nose, the chin, a finely balanced actor's face, spoiled at the moment by being screwed up in a fit of hate, loathing, fear and aggression. McCusker was small, just over five feet tall, but had developed a strong chest and legs, and by the way he was able to keep that metal bar in the air, Montgomerie reckoned he had pretty powerful arms into the bargain.

Two-tone klaxons and yankee-style woofer sirens pierced the air, pretty close too, thought Montgomerie, two or three minutes away at most. McCusker evidently agreed with him. He relaxed his tone and lowered the end of the metal bar to the ground. "OK," he said.

And they fell for it, relaxing their tone and walking into the arc of McCusker's weapon. Piper's left leg was the first to go, splintered at the knee, then McCusker brought the metal bar crashing down on to the ribcage of a startled Montgomerie. The second constable backed up, white-faced, as McCusker jabbed the bar into his solar plexus. McCusker ran a few steps, turned, came back and kicked Montgomerie in the head, before running through a close, into Rutherglen, into the city.

Sergeant Rafferty drove Montgomerie to the hospital, following the ambulance. "Made a right little pig's ear of that, didn't we, sir?" he said.

113

Rory McNulty opened up the West End outpost of McNulty, Spicer and Watson with a ring full of keys and a hefty shove of his shoulder. "These old properties," he said, reaching round the doorway and switching off the burglar alarm.

"Does the customer have to do this?" asked Donoghue, sliding in between the door and the frame, pushing it open.

"No, of course not. It's part of our ever-open door policy. Here, have a card." McNulty reached forward and picked up a card and handed it to Donoghue. On the front the card said that the door was always open 9.00 a.m. to 5.00 p.m. Monday to Friday.

"You should still get it replaced," said Donoghue, sliding the card into his top pocket with every intention of tearing it up as soon as he was away from McNulty's company. "It gives a bad impression if you're dealing in property."

"This is John Spicer's responsibility. I dare say he thinks it's service rather than appearance that matters . . ." He glanced at Donoghue whose eyebrows were slightly raised. "Aye, well, we'll see about that."

114

McNulty opened the safe, took out a small punch of keys and used one to open a filing cabinet. He and King took the files and edgers out of the filing cabinet and laid them on the desks. Donoghue took the opportunity to light his pipe.

"Everything," McNulty said, placing the last ledger on the pile, "relevant to John Spicer's work should be contained in that lot."

"How often are the accounts inspected?" asked Donoghue, opening a ledger and leafing through page after page of numbers, all utterly meaningless to him.

"Annually." McNulty's golden hair shone in the evening sun which streamed through the window. "By the Law Society's accountants."

"So they are inspected quite closely?"

"Oh yes. The Society takes these matters seriously. What are you driving at, Inspector?"

"Would it be possible to falsify those accounts so that the Law Society accountants wouldn't notice any discrepancy?"

"Frankly, yes. It would be extremely difficult but not impossible. No system is

that foolproof and if the accountants really
went to town they'd find something amiss
all right. They're very thorough, but in the
annual audit they are principally concerned
with our ability to cover."

"Cover?" Donoghue flicked his lighter.

"Under the society's rules any firm of
solicitors has to have money in its own
account at any time which is in excess of
the sum of all monies held on the behalf of
clients. I think that's rule 4(l) (a)."

"I see. So it's against the Society's rules to
use clients' monies for personal short-term
investment, for example?"

"Absolutely. We can take money out of
our account and put it where it gets a better
interest but we always have to leave enough
in the current account to pay all our clients
on demand should they all want their money
back on the same day. God forbid that it
should happen, but we have to be ready for
the eventuality."

"And if a solicitor does abuse clients'
money?"

"He's curling on thin ice," replied
McNulty. "He's likely to be struck off or
given a restricted practice licence, to say

nothing of running the risk of arousing the suspicion of you gentlemen."

"Which he has done," said Donoghue.

"But you said this was a murder enquiry?"

"It still is, but John Spicer is linked somehow and it's my guess that it's his shady business practices."

"Allegedly shady," said McNulty shortly.

"Well, shall we see? Would you like to explain the system to us?"

"It's really very simple," said McNulty, and began an explanation which soon left the two police officers in the dark.

"Sorry." Donoghue held up his hand. "You've lost me and I think DC King as well. I wonder if you could look over the books and see if you can find anything to give you cause for concern?"

"Thank you," said McNulty.

Donoghue raised his eyebrows.

"For respecting my professionalism."

"We'll be in the next room," said Donoghue. He and King sat in the reception area and began browsing through magazines and property lists.

"Thoughts?" said Donoghue suddenly, his head buried in a sports magazine.

"Well—" King cleared his throat and put down the copy of *Ideal Home* he had been reading—"I can't really add anything to what you said to McNulty, sir. Bill McGarrigle had an interest in this firm. Spicer seems to be rotten. This guy in Maryhill was in a state of oblivion and when he comes out of oblivion it'll be to a wrecked marriage and no job and no money. He'll blame a lot of that on Spicer screwing him inside out."

"You seem to believe him."

"I still do." Donoghue hadn't lowered his magazine and all King was addressing was the back and front covers behind which a plume of blue smoke was lazily rising.

"Jumping the gun, aren't you?"

"Sir?"

"Remember the small percentage of allegations which result in proven verdicts. Ten, fifteen per cent, is it? I can't recall."

"Somebody had Bill McGarrigle worked over to stop him getting too close to something. That something is either here or where Spicer takes us. I'm convinced of it."

"Good. I like confidence in my officers."

118

He lowered his magazine and relit his pipe. "We'll see what, if anything, McNulty turns up."

They sat and read all the magazines. Donoghue walked out and bought an ounce of tobacco; it would do until he could get some more of his special mix made up. They turned on the lights and began to re-read the magazines. When after three hours McNulty had not emerged from the office Donoghue rose, tapped on the door and walked in to find what if anything McNulty had turned up.

"This will be the end of this firm," he said slowly. He was white-faced and drawn.

"King!" Donoghue called over his shoulder. King joined him. "What have you found, sir?"

"Enough to ruin my life's work." McNulty laid his pen down. At the side of the ledger were sheets of notepaper covered in rough calculations.

"What have you found?" Donoghue asked again, a little firmness creeping into his voice. He switched the light on in the office.

"Thank you. I hadn't realized how dark it had become." McNulty squeezed his eyes.

"Well, gentlemen, I'm afraid you are right. John Spicer is up to something. Basically he's not covered, he is in breach of rule 4(1) (a). If all his clients asked for their money tomorrow he could pay about a third of them. I found these as well." He reached into a drawer and pulled out a folder containing blank bills and wads of blank headed notepaper. He dropped them on to the desk in front of Donoghue. "Building firms, electrical contractors, plumbing companies, glaziers, garages, surveyors—oh, it goes on and on. You name it, there's a bill for a company in that field, all blank, waiting to be filled in."

"How does the system work?" asked Donoghue.

"So far as I can make out, half the house surveys are just not carried out but the client is billed anyway."

"And the rest?" Donoghue tapped the pile of blank bills.

"Who knows, it'll need a thorough investigation, but what I think is happening, judging from the outgoings from John Spicer's accounts, is that work carried out by legitimate firms is billed for under a bogus name."

"With a mark-up?" said Donoghue.

"Yes. A client who is buying a house may well ask us to arrange for it to be rewired, which is often a condition of having a mortgage advanced. John Spicer then seems to contact a reputable firm who do the job and send him their bill for, say, five hundred pounds. He will then make out a bill for the same piece of work under a bogus name, this time for six hundred pounds, and debit the client's account for that amount."

"He pays the legitimate firm and pockets the rest," said Donoghue.

King picked up the yellow pages.

"None of these firms are listed," said McNulty. "It's the first thing I checked."

"How did you find out he can't cover?" asked Donoghue. "Despite this fraud, the figures should balance."

"Simply," said McNulty. "His books don't balance." He spoke slowly, wearily, thought King, who imagined the emotion McNulty must have kept in check as he exposed corruption in that which he had created. "Notwithstanding the fact that he has been milking clients' accounts, his own personal business account is heavily overdrawn, so it means that somewhere among these two hundred-odd accounts there is a sink hole. I've spent most of the last three hours looking for an account that has been consistently credited over the last three months. I took three months as an arbitrary figure, it has no significance, and I found it in the name of Carol McDonald."

"By a large amount?" Donoghue opened his notebook.

"Oh yes, sufficient to bring Mr. Spicer's own account back into the black, and probably a lot of clients' accounts too."

"How long has this been going on?"

"Who knows? Years perhaps. He probably starts juggling money around a few weeks before each audit to make the accounts look good."

"By how much are the accounts short?"

"Well, I don't know exactly, I don't know the extent of the fraud, but the account of Miss Carol McDonald stands at forty-five thousand pounds, or thereabouts."

"Thereabouts?"

"Give or take a thousand. I haven't worked it out to the last penny."

"Is there any indication where the money is going?"

"It's going to a concern called the Fleur

de Lys bar in the centre of the city. According to these documents Miss McDonald is the owner, and according to her accounts it's haemorrhaging badly."

"What address is given?"

"There's two," said McNulty. "The bar is on Coburg Street and Miss McDonald's home address is given as Clematis Cottage, near Strontian, Argyllshire."

"We'll go and see if we can get hold of her at the Fleur de Lys," said Donoghue. "We don't have time to go up to the Highlands."

"You won't get her at either place," said McNulty. "I suggest you try the old school house on the Isle of Bute."

"How do you know that?"

"Because that's where Carol Spicer née McDonald lives with her husband, John Spicer, solicitor, of McNulty, Spicer and Watson. I attended their wedding. Clematis Cottage is their holiday home. I've been there."

6

FAIR Sunday morning filled Scotland with top to bottom sunshine. By 9.00 a.m. in Glasgow it was warm enough for shorts and vests, for sunning in the Botanical Gardens, or packing a few things and away down the water with the kids to the holiday beaches at Ayr or Saltcoats, to Millport or to Arran for a day's walking on the fell, or to the Highlands, or to Loch Lomond for a day's sailing.

Donoghue sat in his Rover outside "P" Division station, and looked up Sauchiehall Street. He had hung his jacket in the car but kept his shirtsleeves down to his wrists, pinned with silver cufflinks. He sat on the leather seat, baked, and listened to Radio 4. Ray Sussock came panting up to the car and tapped on the nearside front window. His jacket was slung over his arm and beads of sweat dripped off his deeply furrowed brow. Donoghue leaned over and unlocked the door. Sussock sat in the passenger seat and began apologizing vociferously for being late.

Donoghue let the clutch in with a jerk, turned on to the Kingston Bridge and joined the M8 Westbound. He nudged the Rover over the seventy mark and drove steadily in the middle lane, occasionally overtaking in the outside lane. Ray Sussock knew Donoghue was angry. He sat silently in the passenger seat, wanting to put on the seat-belt but lacking even the courage to move. He did move, once, while Donoghue was speeding through Gourock: he pulled his tie out of his jacket pocket, buttoned up his shirt and clipped the artificial knot of his tie on to his collar. Donoghue slowed the car at Wemyss Bay railway station, turned sharp right into the ferry-passengers' car park and down the ramp. At the foot of the ramp the 9.30 ferry was preparing to leave, the water was churning under the stern and the tailgate was being raised. Donoghue flashed the headlights and hammered on the horn. The tailgate was lowered and Donoghue drove on board and parked by the side of a coach full of trippers. He switched off the engine and applied the handbrake.

"'Morning, Ray," he said. "That is what is known in the trade as a damn close-run thing."

"Yes, sir," said Sussock, breathing easier.

Donoghue spent the crossing on the upper passenger deck, looking out across the Firth of Clyde, north to the green and brown hills of the Cowal Peninsula, and the bright blue water of the Kyles of Bute where a tanker swung at anchor awaiting a pilot to take her up river. He walked around the wheelhouse and looked south; he could make out Great Cumbrae clearly, but a haze obscured Arran. He breathed deeply, filling his lungs with fresh sea air, leaning on the railings. He watched a one-tonner come about under skilful handling, and put its bows behind the ferry's stern.

Ray Sussock spent the greater part of the crossing in the lounge eating sandwiches and drinking coffee. He was glad he could eat without Donoghue's presence and inevitable questions. It was his breakfast.

He had separated from his wife the previous winter and was still finding living in a bedsitter tough going. It wasn't just that fifty-four wasn't exactly the right time of life to live in the city's netherworld of freaks, oddballs, cast-offs, the mental hospital discharges, all of whom make up the adult population of bedsit land. It was also the difficulty of surviving on his own, of coping with the never ending day-to-day domestic hassles while holding down a job. It was a problem of his which had manifested itself acutely on Fair Sunday morning. He awoke late for his rendezvous with Donoghue and having lacked opportunity to get to the shops or the bank because of the McGarrigle investigation, now found there was no food on his shelf, that someone had pilfered the last of his tea bags and that he had less than two pounds in cash. So here he was, the station eejit, the old boy of the Division, getting respect because of age and nothing else, ten years older than his senior officer, the man with the failed marriage and furtive affair with a WPC and here he was: broke. On top of everything else he had to admit to not getting to a bank before they shut for the Fair. Or had he? The more he thought about it the more he realized his shaky image could not withstand the knock it would have to take if he were to openly admit to being a bad manager by asking to borrow ten quid till Tuesday. The more he thought about it, the more four days did not seem to be such a long stretch, he had a little cash, he could make it, with a little economic rationalization he was sure he could make it.

He left the lounge and went out on to the car deck and was amused to see a seagull hitching a ride on the cab of a lorry. In other circumstances he might have enjoyed the trip, seeing it as a perk of his job, but there were problems weighing on his mind, not the least of which was that it was 10.10 a.m. Sunday, and he now had 53p in cash to last him until the banks opened on Tuesday morning.

He rejoined Donoghue at the Rover as the ferry was docking at Rothesay. They drove off the side ramp and along the wide concrete jetty which separates the two pools of Rothesay harbour, turned left along the front and followed the coast road to the southern most tip of the island, where stood the old school house. Donoghue drove up the driveway. He could still make out the lines of the old village school, a long low roof, a tall square column at one end and an imposing doorway. There, however, the resemblance ended. The windows were expensively stained, the school yard had been landscaped into hanging gardens with running water, leaving just enough room by the door to park a Mercedes station wagon and a Range-Rover, both less than twelve months old. Donoghue parked on the driveway in front of the Range-Rover.

The door was answered by a tall woman wearing jeans and a fisherman's style smock. She had a deep tan, which hadn't been acquired by sitting around in the West of Scotland. There were bracelets by the dozen on each wrist, heavy rocks on her long fingers, and an expensive-looking cigarette smouldering between them.

Sussock noted the woman looking down her nose at him, the way the rich do when they're putting the plebs in their place, usually from an elevated position such as the top of a horse or, as in this case, the top of a flight of steps. Donoghue, for his part, noticed that the cigarette had only recently been lit, probably when she heard the doorbell chime; it hadn't caught properly at the tip and there was not a trace of lipstick on the filter although the woman's lips seemed heavily rouged. Donoghue guessed that underneath the image Super Cool Sophie was all jelly.

Donoghue flashed his I/D. "Police," he said.

The woman raised her eyebrows.

"We'd like to talk to Mr. Spicer," said Donoghue.

"He's not at home."

"When will he be back?"

"Sometime today. He's sailing."

"So he'll be out all day?"

"I can't tell you. He's been out since Friday morning. Do you always work on a Sunday, a public holiday Sunday at that?"

"If it's necessary," said Donoghue. "In this instance, it's necessary that we talk with Mr. Spicer."

"Why?" She put the cigarette to her mouth and drew in the smoke deeply, exhaling in a long thin plume which she directed upwards past the tip of her nose.

"I'm afraid we can't tell you."

"There are no secrets between John and me." There was a note of forced indignation about her voice and Donoghue guessed that there was a whole world of secrets between John and her. She didn't know when he'd be back, she didn't know exactly where he was, and Donoghue doubted that she trusted him.

"Your husband might be back any time, you say?"

"Yes. He could 'phone me in a couple of minutes and ask me to drive down to the harbour and pick him up. But he could 'phone at ten this evening, he may even extend his sail until tomorrow. He doesn't have to work until Tuesday."

"I see. Can I ask which of the cars belong to him?"

"They both do," she replied.

Donoghue looked at her: poor young rich thing, nice home, nice clothes, bangles and rocks and fags but no possessions of her own, there to look pretty, to set the ideal home off just right, having to stay at the post, his to come home to.

"I wonder if we might wait?" asked Donoghue. "In case he should return earlier rather than later."

"If you wish," said the woman. "You may as well come in."

She turned and went into the house. Donoghue and Sussock followed her.

She led them into a room with a sunken lounge in which four light grey deeply upholstered settees surrounded glass-topped coffee table. The room had large window which looked south, ou across the estuary. There was an elevated dining area off to the right, which looked out on to a well-kept lawn at the rear of the house. She sat on a settee and curled her legs up under her. Donoghue sat opposite her and Sussock sat as far into the corner as he could. A Persian cat leapt on to Donoghue's lap. Both its presence and its sub-species hardly surprised him.

"That's Maxwell Eddison," said the woman by means of introduction. Then changing the subject, "We often get policemen calling on us."

"Do you?" replied Donoghue. He put her at about twenty-six or twenty-seven and provisionally assessed her as being bored to tears.

"I don't know what they come for, to talk about John's cases, I expect. He usually talks to them in the second sitting-room."

"The second sitting-room?"

"John won't have a television in here and so we have a few old chairs and a set in a small room just back there." She waved a well-manicured hand above her head.

"We're investigating a murder," said Donoghue suddenly. It was a gamble to say that, a risk, but none the less he took it. He was interested in her reaction.

"A murder," she said and raised her eyebrows. She stuck the posh fag in her mouth.

"Uh-huh." Donoghue began to stroke the cat.

"One of John's cases?"

"Probably."

"Probably?"

"We won't know for certain until we talk to your husband." Then he took another gamble. "He doesn't keep any documents in the house, does he?"

"Nothing to do with his practice. Just odds and ends to do with the business."

"The business?"

"We run a pub, the Fleur de Lys. At least, John runs it." She laid the cigarette on the ashtray which was big enough to turn into an indoor water garden. "If things go badly then the creditors can't get their hands on the house," she explained, "because it's in my name. The house, that is."

"Ah," said Donoghue. "Is it going badly?"

133

"I really don't know. I'm not privy to such things."

"It certainly seems to be paying." Donoghue looked about him. "If you don't mind my saying so."

The woman smiled. "We haven't had the pub for very long. The money for the house came from John's practice. I don't know how well the pub's going, John hasn't been looking too pleased at the moment, but he wouldn't tell me either way."

"You said there were no secrets between you."

"Ah, I meant of a personal nature. John rarely discusses his work with me. Frankly, I don't particularly want to discuss it."

"Do you talk much to your husband?"

"I don't see him much to talk with. To get to his work he's got to get the seven-thirty ferry and he doesn't get back until late. Sometimes eight at night. He eats dinner and then retires."

Retires. That word somehow forced itself. "It's a long day," Donoghue observed.

"John thinks it's worth it so that he can be on the island at weekends, right away from Glasgow. We used to live in the city, near the Botanical Gardens, but John always felt on top of his work. He does a lot of conveyancing, you see, and when he took me for a walk on Sundays he'd get upset because he'd see all the houses that he was conveying. So we moved here."

"It must have taken quite some effort to get the house in this sort of order."

"About four months."

"Is that all?"

"Oh, John hired some men and they did it all. John didn't even have to lift a hammer to a nail." Then she smiled as though that was a big achievement. "Would you care for some coffee?"

She carried the tray into the room with a good poise and set it down neatly on the table. The tray was silver, the cups and saucers were good china, the coffee was cheap instant stuff with boiling water slopped over it. But at least she hadn't apologized for it being the maid's day off.

Donoghue sipped the coffee and winced. It was strong and acid. "And yourself, Mrs. Spicer, are you happy to live on the island?"

"Well, yes." Mrs. Spicer had curled herself back on to the settee. She hadn't lit another cigarette and Donoghue thought she was beginning to relax and possibly even enjoy the opportunity to chat, since the two police officers, were, by her own admission, probably the first human contact she had had in two days. "One can't have it all ways."

"Which ways do you miss?" asked Donoghue, not slow to respond to her invitation to ask her about herself.

"I enjoyed the city; there was a sense of belonging."

"You feel remote here?"

"Well, John likes it but I miss our flat in Hillhead."

"You certainly seem close to your husband," Donoghue commented.

"Oh, we're very close, John and I." She reached forward and picked up her packet of cigarettes and selected one. Donoghue took the lighter from his pocket and lit it, extending his arm over the coffee table. She leant towards him and lit her cigarette, looking at him with large brown eyes as she withdrew.

"Have you been married a long time?" Donoghue took his pipe from his pocket.

"Four years."

"How long have you lived here?"

"Two years, two years and a few months. I forget exactly. You know how the months seem to melt into each other."

Donoghue nodded sympathetically.

"I still do miss the city if I have to be honest." She glanced over her shoulder towards the garden. "But one must stay with one's husband, mustn't one?"

"Oh, marriage is not to be undertaken lightly," agreed Donoghue. Mustn't one; one is sounding untrue to oneself. "Did you grow up in a town?"

"Oh yes. Glasgow, as a matter of fact; in the north of the city." She raised her eyebrows slightly. North of the city, somewhere between Bearsden and Royston, a bit nearer Royston.

She had worked hard, Donoghue knew she had worked damn hard but she hadn't quite made it. He was a street kid himself, he'd got out via Glasgow University, but roots were roots, they stayed with you, and he could recognize another child of the cobbles and the high kerbstones. Carol Spicer, it seemed, had got out by marrying into money and Donoghue saw her six or eight years previously, Carol McDonald, looking demure in the smooth bars, flashing her eyes at the accountants and under-managers and the second-hand car salesmen. Now she was here and she was here to stay, but her chemistry was still wrong, she had the image but not the substance, like cheap coffee carelessly made and served in expensive china.

"I grew up in Sighthill," said Donoghue. He threw that one in to test the reaction.

It was a curious reaction. She tried to sniff at his past like she thought she ought, but it didn't come off. She managed to pull her head back slightly and to wrinkle her nose, but the effect was spoiled by the look in her eye as she suddenly saw Donoghue as someone who has also been there, someone who understands, a fellow traveller.

The room was silent. She looked at Donoghue, he looked down at the cat curled up at the side of him, loving his hand on its ears. Ray Sussock sat quietly in the corner.

"Those were tough streets," she reached out, breaking the silence.

"I dare say an outsider would find them tough," he replied, running his forefinger up and down the cat's nose. "It wasn't so bad if you belonged." There followed another silence and Donoghue knew he was caressing her nerve-endings with a feather.

"If you belonged," she said.

Donoghue grunted.

"Did you belong?" she pressed him.

He grunted again, still looking at the cat.

"I never thought I belonged." He knew by the way she said it that it was a hard thing for her to say. It came out like a confession.

"Why was that?" Donoghue spoke softly. Tell me, my child.

"Well—" she pulled hard on the cigarette—"I felt I belonged in Hillhead but that was the West End; I feel comfortable here as well. But those streets, the Saracen, was—well, really there was nothing for us."

"Us!"

"My sister and me."

"I see."

"We both said we'd get out some day, but there's horrible pressures to keep you there, from your mates, you know?"

"Aye," said Donoghue, helping her to relax into street speak.

"You get spat at, stabbed with spike-handled combs because you're taken for posh."

139

"You got out all right in the end, though."

"In the end. We got flats in Hillhead, really cramped. My sister went first and shared with some girls, then I left and got a flat of my own. The West End was rare. I enjoyed it."

"Good."

"The trick was to keep your legs together."

"What!" Donoghue was startled by her statement.

"Aye. That was the trick right enough. We thought it out one night, me and Anne. Open your legs too easily and you're anybody's and you end up with a ned. Keep 'em together and you build up a—a—Anne had a word for it—" she moved her hand in a circular motion. "Aye, a mysticism. That way you got the right sort of guy."

"Like a solicitor?"

"So what's wrong with that? It worked, didn't it? I got out, didn't I?" She drew angrily on her cigarette. "So I'm a kept woman; it's better'n being in a council high rise with kids and a man who is no good. This world is for surviving in. To survive you need money. I'm surviving."

140

"That's a simple enough philosophy." Donoghue lit his pipe.

"I may seem hard but I've done better than any I was at school with. I went back one day and walked along the streets. They didn't recognize me but I saw them. I couldn't believe it, they were as old as me, but they'd aged, got shapeless, and the worry on their faces and the kids at their feet! I've done all right and I don't think it matters that I don't love my husband; they don't love their husbands. It's an arrangement that suits both me and John."

"Has your sister done as well as you?"

"Don't be so bloody sarcastic!" She ground her cigarette into the ashtray and then added. "My sister is dead."

"I'm sorry."

"No, you're not. But it doesn't matter. She was murdered five years ago, five years last Friday. There's a wee rat called Gilheaney doing time for it. He got fifteen years. It wasn't enough. I always swore I'd kill him when he got out, but now he's just ceased to exist as far as I'm concerned."

"Gilheaney . . . five years ago last Friday . . ." Donoghue said to himself, slowly realizing something.

141

"That's right. She was knifed. The papers called it the Fair Friday Murder."

"FFM," said Donoghue.

"Sorry?" She inclined her head and raised her eyebrows, slipping back into acquired habits.

"Oh, nothing, nothing," he said. "Yes, I remember the case quite well although I wasn't actually involved."

Ray Sussock sat with an empty coffee cup on his lap and said nothing. He had been in charge of the police investigation and the resulting submission to the Procurator Fiscal which had put Jack "the Granite" Gilheaney inside, despite a not guilty plea which went all the way to the Court of Criminal Appeal in Edinburgh.

Donoghue wondered whether the death of her sister had hurt her badly or whether she had weathered the storm, had hardened by then. It seemed to Donoghue that her survival code in this world of hard knocks lay in the philosophy of getting shot of as much emotion as possible.

"Were you close to your sister?"

"Not very."

Surprise, surprise. Donoghue patted the cat.

"But it worked out, you know, good out of the bad, because that's how I met John."

"Oh?"

"Anne worked for John, she was his secretary and receptionist in the office in the city centre, before John moved out to Byres Road. She had a lovely telephone voice."

"Really?"

"Yes. After she was murdered John kept coming round to my flat. He was very supportive, not emotionally supportive, but supportive in a practical way. He helped me sort out Anne's effects, I was her only relative by then, and John was the only person who could advise me. That's how we got close . . . well . . ."

"I see."

"But he did help a great deal, you know, he told me what to keep of Anne's and what I could chuck out . . ."

"Sorry." Donoghue held up his hand. "He told you what to keep and what to sling."

"With regard to her papers, not her personal belongings, her clothes, her records, but her papers. She had collected a lot of legal-looking papers, statements, columns of figures. John advised me about them; in fact he said I could burn the lot, so we did. Anyway he was getting middle-aged and I was a young and pretty virgin, he was rolling in it and I was broke. We were married a year later. I made him wait until after the wedding until he got anything. It didn't bother him, he was screwing around like a rabbit throughout our engagement and he still got a white wedding to please his old mum."

"Are you happy with that?"

"Aye, like I said, I've got comforts and food and heating and no big demands. Any marriage is a form of gaol sentence, so why not make your cell as comfortable as possible?" She held up her left hand but Donoghue was unsure exactly which was the wedding band. "There's probably a female on the boat right now, or maybe he's taken a brace this time."

"That doesn't bother you?"

"Not unless he comes home and gives me a dose. He hasn't so far."

They left when Donoghue sensed that the conversation was getting circular. On the steps Donoghue said he might well be calling back, probably tomorrow.

"Do that," said Carol Spicer, and smiled in a way which unnerved Donoghue. As he turned he noticed stickers in the rear windows of both Spicer's cars. "How is he disabled?" he asked.

"He's got a small right arm," she said, still smiling, but having regained her middle-class-woman-at-the-door-of-her-home pose. "He said it just stopped growing when he was about twelve years old. He has no strength in that arm or that hand. But it's never bothered me."

On Rothesay front Donoghue suggested a lager. They left the Rover and inspected three bars and, finding each packed to bursting point, abandoned the idea, much to Sussock's relief; he had walked alongside Donoghue clutching his 53p in a clammy hand. Instead they walked around the harbour while waiting for the ferry. As they turned back towards the ferry terminal they noticed a white sailing cruiser nudging its way gently into the yacht basin. There was a young blonde woman in white jersey and white slacks coiling a rope on the foredeck, and a second woman, also blonde and dressed in white, was securing the mainsail to the boom. At the tiller was a thin middle-aged man with a narrow face which seemed frozen in a permanent grin. He held the tiller with his left hand and controlled the throttle with a foot control. His small right arm hung useless.

"He seems to be the sort that likes them in uniform as well," said Sussock. "Will we interview him now?"

"No," said Donoghue. "He's not going anywhere and before I see him I want to have a look at the Gilheaney file, and pick your brains about the matter. There's something sinister here, Ray."

7

MONTGOMERIE knocked three times on the door and was about to knock for a fourth time, although by encouraging one of the constables to use his shoulder instead of the palm of his hand, when the door was opened with a gentle, half-apologetic click. In the doorway stood a thin, drawn, ashen-faced woman with black hair. She blinked at Montgomerie and at the two constables behind him.

"Is he in?" Montgomerie snarled.

"No, he's away," said the woman, shaking her head. "He'll no be back, sure he won't."

"Where's he away to?" asked Montgomerie.

"Dunno."

"You're Mrs. McCusker, aye?"

"Aye."

"How old are you?"

The woman looked at him.

"McCusker's got to be at least

147

thirty-seven," said Donoghue. "You don'
look to be much over seventeen."

"I'm thirty-two," she replied thinly.

Then he could see the tiredness in he
eyes and the odd grey hair, but she was s
small and fragile; like a little bird. "An
he's not here?" he said.

"You should know, you've had a man ir
a car out front all night. He should've com
up and waited in here. I'd have made him
cup of tea."

Montgomerie started to tell her not to ge
too wise and then realized that she was being
serious. So he said again, "He's not here?"

"No."

"Then you won't mind if we take a lool
around?"

The woman stepped aside in a gestur
of total acquiescence to authority
Montgomerie and the two constables walkec
into her home. Montgomerie steppec
lightly, his ribs were badly bruised and he
had suffered the additional indignity o
having them strapped up tightly by Fiona
They hurt like hell all the time except the
brief instant when his left foot touched the
ground, when it felt like he was stopping
the iron bar all over again.

The McCusker household had a musty sort of smell about it. The living-room seemed well fitted out, three-piece suite, television, hi-fi, sideboard, but a close look revealed that it was all old second-hand junk that a labourer could pay for with a good day's wages. The bedroom was the real nitty-gritty, an old three-quarter bed with blankets and sheets, clothes strewn over an old settee which had been pushed against the wall under the window. The kitchen had a yellow formica-topped table, two stools, a sink full of dirty mugs and plates, a working surface with a packetful of cornflakes and a bottle with some milk inside.

"Fallen on hard times, have you?" said Montgomerie when he went back to the living-room.

"Bernie's got a plan," she said, not really looking at Montgomerie. After a while people in authority get so they don't have faces or personalities, they're just the polis, or the social, or the welfare, or the factor, or the gas or the 'lectric. They're all one and you just say "sir", so after a pause she added, "sir".

"Like when his ship comes in," said Montgomerie. "Only it hasn't got anywhere in the last twenty years and both of us know it's not likely to get anywhere in the next twenty."

She looked at him and then looked down at the carpet. Blue, and burnt here and there with cigarette ends.

"So why don't you tell us where he is?"

"Don't know where he is."

"This his?" Montgomerie picked up a black cape which was hung over the back of a chair.

"Aye." She looked at it and then looked back at the carpet, maybe to see if it's still there, thought Montgomerie.

"I'm taking it away with me." Montgomerie handed the cloak to one of the constables.

"He'll not like that," protested the woman, the city waif. "It's his thing, like. He got it off a market stall." She looked again at the carpet.

"Well, if he wants it back tell him to enquire at the desk of DC Montgomerie, the police station, Charing Cross, Glasgow G3." He turned to leave and then he too glanced at the carpet and then at the furniture on the carpet. It was all junk, but heavy junk, solid bits of wood, as though it hadn't been bought so much for furnishing but to hold the carpet in place. He checked the edge of the carpet: it was fastened by nails hammered in at six-inch intervals.

Naturally they ripped it up.

Under the carpet they found an area of loose floorboards, under which they found: four twelve-bore shotguns with barrels and butts sawn off, twenty-five twelve-bore cartridges, two. 38 Service revolvers with six rounds of ammunition each, three pounds of gelignite in commercial blasting sticks, five detonators, fifty feet of fuse wire, black masks and balaclavas. In one of the wardrobes they found six combat jackets, three pickaxe handles and two jemmies.

"Going to knock over the Bank of Scotland, are you?" said Montgomerie to the city waif who was chewing her knuckles. "Get your coat, you're coming for a ride."

Cleopatra McCusker was taken from the rear seat of the police car and down to one of the interview rooms in the basement of the police station. She sat on the chair and began to shiver although the temperature in the room was a comfortable 65°F. A stout policewoman stood in the room with her but said nothing.

Montgomerie signed in and went up to the CID rooms. In his pigeonhole was a print-out from the Police National Computer. It read:

McCUSKER BERNARD—NO TRACE

"That's all I need," he said, walking over to his desk and sitting down.

"What is all you need, my son?" asked King from behind the *Sunday Standard*.

"No trace on that ned that filled in Bill McGarrigle. And bruised my ribs."

"Not to mention PC Piper's fractured leg." King laid the paper on his desk and peered closely at the newsprint. "The spirit of Scotland, strange to say, one word, three letters."

"Don't you have anything better to do?" Montgomerie reached forward and picked up the 'phone on his desk. He consulted an internal directory and dialled a two figure number.

"I'm waiting on Fabian and Ray Sussock coming back. They went to the Isle of Bute this morning."

"And they call that work."

"It's rum," said King.

"It's jam," said Montgomerie, holding

152

the 'phone to his ear. "Getting a trip to Bute on the company's expense, that's jam."

"Scotland's spirit is rum." King scribbled with his ballpoint.

"I thought it was supposed to be whisky."

"It's a double meaning, you know, spirit of the soul, or didn't you know you were supposed to be dour?"

"Hello, collater?" Montgomerie picked up his pen and held it over his notebook. "DC Montgomerie, request information on one Bernard McCusker, probably known as Bernie, of 224 Carrick Road, Rutherglen. Yes, I'll hold, thank you." He held for a moment and then began writing. When he had finished scribbling he thanked the collater and replaced the receiver. He read over what he had written.

McCusker Bernard, Bernie. Alias: Neutron John
No age, no employment, no previous.
Known associate of Sam "the Weight" Dolan, "Jug" McLintock and "Steamroller" Forbes.
(PNC data on above).
All criminal associates of Phil and Tiny

153

Jardine.
Case live to DC King.

"Eh, gringo," said Montgomerie, looking at King.

King grunted.

"Gringo," Montgomerie said again. "Maybe we can do business, exchange a leetle information as we say in Mehico?"

King glanced up from the crossword. "You slay me," he said drily.

"I want only information, compadre."

"Such as?"

"Whatever you can tell me about two banditos yclept Jardine."

"Jardine?"

"Si, el Jardino."

"The Jardine brothers. Phil and Tiny. Tiny's the older and the heavy, Phil is the brains." King put his ballpoint on his desk, leaned backwards and took a file from his filing cabinet. He laid the file on his desk and patted it. On a scale of one to ten for thickness Montgomerie would have given it nine point five. "Oh, there's more than this," said King cheerfully. "This one is marked, Jardine, brackets, Overspill. You should see the first file. What we've got on

154

the Jardines would make a Mafia Kangaroo Court ooze with satisfaction, but it does not impress our own dear Fiscal's office."

"Let me have the condensed version."

"The Jardines are serious hoods. They're as heavy duty as anything in this city, and have been behind most of the big jobs north of the river in the last ten years. They seem to operate a fall guy system, because all the neds who get sizable terms for armed robbery or robbery with violence couldn't think their way out of George Square. But they pull the job efficiently, like programmed robots, and don't get picked up until days or weeks later, by which time all the money has vanished without trace. Like I said, everything points to Phil Jardine being the brains and cuddly Tiny being the recruiting sergeant, but things have moved a bit since the witch-hunting days, we can't just point a finger any more. Anyway, Fabian Donoghue wants them badly, so does Findlater, and so on up to the top of the hierarchy of the great organization of which you and I are but humble servants. Our perennial problem is that evidence and the Jardines seem mutually exclusive."

"You're working on them at the moment?"

"Not actively, my son. Just watching them, and keeping my ears open. Not a dicky-bird for a wee while, though. The last job that could be put down to them with any degree of certainty was the wages snatch at the north entrance to the Clyde tunnel."

"They rammed it with a car with a railway sleeper sticking out over the bonnet and cut their way in with a chain saw."

"That's the one. Took close on a quarter of a million in just under a hundred and twenty seconds, left their car and the van blocking the road, took off in a second car and disappeared into the south side."

"Not bad pay for two minutes' work."

"About sufficient to keep the Jardines in a manner to which they have become accustomed for about twelve months. They put some aside to pay off the fall guys after they've done their bird. I think they're regrouping: Tiny's been seen in the Jardine bars with some up and coming neds."

"They run bars as well?"

"Uh-huh. I reckon they put their illegitimate gains into legitimate businesses.

You've seen the chain of gin bins around the city, all called Delayney's?"

"Aye."

"They own them."

"Do they now. I've been in one of them a couple of times. Cheap wine, hard whisky and short measures of both."

"That's the unmistakable Jardine touch," said King. "Downbeat bars but they pay, and enable the Jardines to live in palatial splendour. Phil is out in the foothills of the Campsies, in a big Victorian house with stables and his own private curling pond which, when it melts in the spring, provides trout fishing. Phil is married with a couple of daughters whom he's trying to unload on to any two members of the respectable business community, but nobody wants to know on account of the fact that they're spoiled rotten. Tiny's pad is out by Barrhead. Have you driven from Paisley to Barrhead and noticed a long low bungalow standing in a field? It has a frontage of at least a hundred feet with a white five-barred gate at the entrance to the drive."

"Don't tell me that's Tiny's."

"Afraid so. It's got a western name, the 'double J' or the 'J. J.' or something like that. Anyway, it's known to all in the syndicate as 'the ranch'. One end of the building is given over to a gymnasium because Tiny's into a physical culture kick and, not to put too fine a point on it, he's built like a brick shithouse. He doesn't have his younger brother's stability, Tiny likes his women young and usually has not less than three in the house at any one time."

"And you think the clan is gathering again, about to mount a raid on the defenceless hamlet of G?"

"I think so. Like I said, Tiny's been seen recruiting. I think he's got three, Dolan, McLintock and Forbes. They're all neds with Pc's for violence. If the Jardines follow the usual pattern a bank or something will be knocked over, Dolan, McLintock and Forbes will be collared because they're too stupid to avoid it. Scanty evidence will link them to the Jardine brothers, who will of course have a cast-iron alibi as to their whereabouts at the time of the raid and will never have met or had any contact with anybody connected with the raid. The money naturally will never be recovered, but only a matter of weeks later the Jardines will be spending like they've had a pools win and another bar will open and add to the growing Delayney chain."

"The neds will get ten years plus but because they've only been small timers before they might be able to get away with patter on the lines of 'I was just a hot head getting in out of my depth,' get transferred to an open prison after four or five years, stick to the rules like superglue, be very contrite and get paroled after another couple of years."

"Which is not a hard ride."

"Of course not, and when they do step outside they suddenly come into money. If they're married, their wives don't appear to live the hand to mouth Supplementary Benefit existence of most prisoners' wives."

"Got it sewn up, haven't they?" Montgomerie tapped the notepad on his desk. "I've got another name for you. He'll be in the ned category, sub category, apprentice. One 'Neutron John'."

"Neutron John," sighed King, writing in the file. "Don't know how they get those names."

"Real name McCusker, Bernard."

King stopped writing. "He . . ."

"Murdered Bill McGarrigle, bruised my ribs and smashed Piper's knee."

"What's the connection with the Jardines?"

So Montgomerie told him that the collater had McCusker listed as a known associate of Dolan, *et al.* He also told him about the guns and explosives found under McCusker's floorboards and about the pickaxe handles and jemmies found in the wardrobe belonging to the self-same felon.

There are two basic methods of conducting an interrogation. One involves the use of electrodes, saturated towels and coshes. The other method involves the subject being left alone in a small, sparsely furnished room, or sometimes left in the company of a stony-faced and totally mute constable. The subject's anxiety level then begins to rise and when it has reached a point where the subject is screaming inside his skull, a police officer enters the room, sits down, opens a packet of fags and smiles, effectively saying "Let's be friends." By the time King and Montgomerie entered the interview room Cleopatra McCusker was tearing out her hair.

Montgomerie sat in front of her and took out a packet of cigarettes. She snatched one and pushed it between her lips with trembling fingers. Casually Montgomerie selected a cigarette for himself and lit it, then extended the match half way across the table. Cleopatra McCusker leaned forward to meet it and, catching her fag, inhaled deeply and then sighed, exhaling the smoke. To King it was not unlike watching someone come up for air after a long time under water, or watching a junkie get his fix.

"I didn't know about they guns and things," she said before Montgomerie had opened his pad.

Coolly he opened his notepad and turned to the first blank page. He took the tip from his ballpoint, looked at Cleopatra McCusker, smiled and said, "Yes, you did."

"Don't know much."

"All right. Tell us what you do know and then tell us the rest."

"He brought the guns in last week," she said, burning down the cigarette as though it was stuck in a furnace flue.

"Alone?"

"Aye."

"How did he get them to your house?"

"He had this van."

"Who looked over his flat to check it was an OK plank?"

The first silence.

"How long did he say he'd be keeping the armoury?" Montgomerie passed on quickly to keep her talking. Nice easy questions. For the moment.

"Two weeks."

"When exactly did he bring them in?"

"Last week."

"Today's Sunday, hen. So did he bring them in after last Sunday or before?"

"Before, sir."

King winced. Sir. Dinna anger the laird.

"How long before?"

"A few days."

"So you've had them for close on two weeks?"

She nodded and dogged her fag in the plastic ashtray. She screwed it down in to the tray even though she had an inch of good smoke left and by the time she'd finished grinding with her bony hand the cigarette was just a pile of shredded filter and paper and weed.

"You don't of course have any idea what the guns were to be used for?"

162

She shook her head. Of course.

"That's what 'Jug' McLintock said." King spoke matter of factly to Montgomerie.

"Uh-huh," grunted Montgomerie. "We'll give him another hour before we go back."

Cleopatra McCusker's eyes flashed backwards and forwards between the two officers.

"Not feeling too happy?" asked Montgomerie.

"Been inside one of these rooms before, have you?" asked King.

The woman nodded.

"Tell us. We'll be checking anyway."

"Och, shoplifting, breach of the peace," said the woman, shaking her head.

"It's a big step up from that to armed robbery." Montgomerie tapped the ash from his cigarette into the ashtray and logged the remains. "Sure you're ready for it?"

"I'm not involved."

"You're in up to your ears, hen," said Montgomerie.

"Aiding and abetting, conspiracy to rob," said King. "We've been talking to Jug."

"I'd like another cigarette," said th
woman.

"I'd like a statement," growle
Montgomerie.

"Away tae hell."

"When did you first meet up with Ju
and Steamroller?" asked King.

"In the Fleur de Lys," said the woma
before she could stop herself.

"Yes, we know where," said King. "Th
time confuses us."

"I don't remember."

"Yes, you do. You went along wit
Neutron one night. You met up with Ju
and Steamroller and another guy." Kin
looked at the ceiling and clicked his finger:
a man trying to recall something. "Oh yeal
that's it. Some ned called Sam Dolan. H
had a handle—'heavy' or something."

"The Weight," said the woman. "The
call him 'the Weight', so they do."

Montgomerie thought she was standin
up well, very anxious, a few tears but no
distraught like some women would be. Sh
had the body of a Belsen inmate bu
mentally she was tough, tough, tough.

Still, they were getting there, slowly
King took a packet of cigarettes from h

acket and offered her one. "Have a smoke, hen," he said gently. Montgomerie took he cue and slammed his hand down hard against the table so suddenly and violently hat the woman jumped backwards. "Right, Madam McCusker," he snarled. "No more annying around. Your man's got you in up o your ears, you're using your flat as a weapons store, you're planning something, omething big. What? When?"

"Don't know," she screamed. "Don't loody know nothing, nothing."

"Yes, you do."

She started sniffling. Then she stopped herself and glared at him. Defiant. It was her against Montgomerie. So far as she was concerned neither the WPC nor King were n the room.

"You're in deep."

"So!"

He stood up and leaned over her.

She said, simply, "Sit down."

"When I come back," growled Montgomerie, his face close to hers, "when I ome back you and me will have a talk. Without an audience." He walked out of he room, pulling the door shut behind him.

"He has a bit of a temper," said King,

sitting in the chair previously occupied by Montgomerie. "Would you like tha cigarette now?"

"Aye," sniffed the woman wiping he eyes.

"It's a tough life you've got." He handec her a cigarette and struck a match. He li one for himself. "I mean, you're not exactl rolling in clover in your flat from what hear and Neutron's not the sort of man woman of your age could do with." He pulled on his cigarette. "Maybe he can thril the young ones but when a woman is in he thirties she needs a bit of stability, a bit o reliability, someone who can help her builc a home."

"Aye." She smiled and nodded. The masochistic resignation to life's lot: play the hand you're dealt and don't argue with the big dealer.

"How long have you been with him?"

"Ten years, on and off."

"Knocks you about, aye?"

"Oh, aye," in a tone which suggested i would be abnormal if he didn't.

"Kids?"

"No," she said after a short silence which King thought meant that there wer probably two or three young McCuskers currently thriving in a foster home.

"Much life of your own?"

"What do you mean?"

"Friends of your own, ever get a night out with the girls, get to the bingo?"

"Away, me? No."

"Not ever?"

"I'm to be inside waiting on him coming home. I only get out with him. He has the keys."

"He takes you out for a drink?"

"Sometimes."

"Not anywhere nice, though. I mean, the Fleur de Lys is hardly a ladies' bar." King pulled on his fag.

"I've been in worse."

"Like the Delayney bars?"

"Aye." She drew hard on the cigarette, but when she exhaled only a little smoke came out of her nostrils. It gave King an indication of the state of her lungs. "I mean, you can sit down in the Fleur; in Delayney's you stand in the sawdust and listen to the men talk."

"That's right." King nodded. "Come to think of it, it was fairly slack when I was in the Fleur. Mind you, that was mid-afternoon."

"It's slack all the time," she said. "He can't make it pay."

"Why?"

"Don't know. There's always somebody working, though. On the building, I mean. I think it's falling down."

"You sound like you know the owner. Neutron making his way up the social ladder, is he?"

"Och, he likes to think he is. He's just a wee nobody. Takes a drink with the head man and he thinks he's one of the directors."

"You can see through it all, aye?"

"Aye, buttering him up to play their game. Have a wee drink, son, loading up the gun for Neutron to fire it."

"That'd be Phil Jardine." King took a drag on his cigarette and looked up at the light-bulb.

"Aye, that's him. He's better than his brother. Tiny's a bastard."

"So he is," said King.

"You know him?" She looked at him.

"Oh, aye, know of him anyway. He's ruined a lot of people, sent them to the gaol and got fat on their efforts."

"Aye, but he's looked after them."

"Neutron told you that, did he?"

"No. Phil Jardine."

"The man himself."

"Aye. He came over to us when we were in the Fleur. Phil Jardine was with the others, talking to the owner of the bar, Spicer, him with the funny wee arm, talking away like, and Phil Jardine came over to us and told us that it should go all right on Tuesday but if it didn't he'd see us all right."

"He said that."

"Aye, that he'd be looking after us."

"Don't believe a word of it."

"No?"

"No. Anybody who gets involved with the Jardines ends up broke and in a mess. All busted up."

"They get to do the job, but they're taken care of."

"I know, Phil Jardine told you. You've seen where he lives, have you?"

"Aye." She nodded.

That was an unexpected bonus.

"So how's he going to keep a place like that going and look after all the wives and women of all the guys doing bird on his account?"

"Maybe it's pretty big."

"It is large enough."

"Aye, it's no splendid, but what's he got in here?"

"Enough," said King.

"Four rooms, maybe five." She dragged on her cigarette. "Those West End flats are big but his is falling down like the Fleur. And it's not all that well furnished, just a few sticks and bits of carpet."

"Aye, but it stills costs," said King. "What do you think of Spicer, the guy with the little arm? You don't sound as though you like him?"

"No. He's all . . ." she shivered.

"He doesn't turn you on."

"No. I don't fancy him at all. He fancies himself as a ladies' man and he's always got a young girl somewhere near."

"You don't have to talk to him, though. I mean, he was over there with the Jardines and Neutron and Jug and the rest, planning it out, and you were away in the corner. That's not so bad."

"No, it wasn't. I was with Jug's missus and Steamroller's girl. We were having a blether. That's who Phil Jardine was talking to, us, all of us three. He came over and said we'd be all right after they'd done the job if the polis showed up."

"I see. He told all three of you?"

"Aye, that's how I believed him. I'd be a bit suspicious if he told just me." She smiled. King smiled back. "I didn't get near that guy with the little arm that night but Neutron brought him to our house a few nights later. He had a look round."

"At the floorboards and carpets?"

"I suppose so. I didn't see. I was sent to the bedroom."

"That was a few days before the guns came?"

"Aye, how did you know that? Did Jug tell you?"

"Maybe. I know quite a bit really."

"But you don't know about the job. The other man said you didn't."

"We don't know everything," said King. "We know a little."

"You're a good man," said Cleopatra McCusker, smiling. "You're good to talk to. You can come round and see me, you know, afterwards."

"Dare say we'll be seeing each other again," said King. "What I can tell you is that the job will be pulled in Glasgow."

"Aye, in Maryhill." She smiled. "Bet you don't know where?"

"Queens Cross," said King confidently. But it was a shot in the dark. "I went there yesterday to see a guy."

"Aye." The woman sounded disappointed. "The Bank on the corner, the little hut thing. How did you know?"

"How did you know, that's more to the point?" said King.

"Neutron told me when he was drunk," she said. "See all the things he's going to do with that money."

"I bet he also told you not to tell anyone," said King.

The WPC cleared her throat. Cleopatra McCusker went white and began to cry again, only this time she didn't just weep, she bawled and hammered her tiny fists on the table.

Montgomerie was waiting in the corridor, leaning against the wall smoking a cigarette. He fell into step with Richard King as he walked away from the interview room.

"How did it go?" asked Montgomerie.

"Gold dust, my son," said King. "Pure gold dust."

It was Fair Sunday, midday.

172

8

FAIR Sunday 1.30 p.m.

Donoghue, Sussock, King and Montgomerie sat in Donoghue's office. They were dressed in their shirt-sleeves and all except Donoghue had unclipped their ties. The windows were open but the temperature in the room was in the high 80's. The blue fug from Donoghue's pipe didn't help either; it hung in layers, rising slowly. King had written up an account of his interview with Cleopatra McCusker in a neat longhand and had had it photocopied for distribution. While King was writing up his report Montgomerie was in a bar, having been driven there by the heat in search of a lager or two. The meeting caught him unawares and he reported his search for Bernie McCusker, alias Neutron John, sucking ferociously on a mint as he spoke. Donoghue gave a succinct verbal account of his meeting with Carol Spicer née McDonald. Sussock was silent for most of the meeting, his thoughts being continually dragged back to the thirty-six hours stretching in front of him and the 53p in his pocket with which to survive. Donoghue was the last to speak. He ended his feedback by re-filling his pipe and asking for comments.

"Bill McGarrigle didn't know what he was stumbling on," said Montgomerie.

"Or maybe he did," replied Donoghue, flicking his lighter. "Maybe he knew fine that it would make him as a journalist. Anyway, this isn't getting us very far. What have we got, a solicitor who's as crooked as the Highland Way, who's involved with organized crime and who may or may not be party to a bank raid which may or may not go ahead now we have the hardware. He's also linked with the murder of Bill McGarrigle and the Fair Friday murder of five years ago."

"Pops up in all the wrong places, does Spicer," said King.

Donoghue grunted and tapped the sheet of paper in front of him. "No prints on any of the hardware and all the serial numbers of the guns had been filed off, the ones inside the mechanism as well as the ones on the stock."

"That more than anything indicates professionalism," said King.

"Absolutely," agreed Donoghue. "So where do we go from here? I think I know but I'm not going to do all the work." He paused. The group was silent. "Well, firstly then, will the bank raid go ahead on Tuesday a.m.?"

"Odd day to have a raid," said Montgomerie. "Friday a.m. I could understand, but Tuesday . . ." He shook his head.

"It's not just any Tuesday." Donoghue was irritated by Montgomerie's lack of insight.

"It's their first working day after the Fair," growled Sussock. "There'll be big withdrawals on Tuesday morning because all the punters will be broke."

"That's right," said Donoghue, "and there will be less police on duty than there were on Fair Friday. It must be one of the few days of the year when big withdrawals are expected and when police cover is only normal. It's my guess that, if they have a secondary supply of weapons, the raid will go ahead."

"We can't ignore the possibility," said

King. "Especially as the bank they've earmarked is an easy one to knock over."

"Oh?" Donoghue raised his eyebrows.

"Yes. It's a temporary structure sitting on the corner of a piece of wasteground. Little more than a garden shed."

"It does indeed sound likely," agreed Donoghue. "So we'll assume the raid is on. Now McCusker alias Neutron John and his pals are already in some sort of safe house in the West End. We have to locate them."

"Big place to cover," said Montgomerie.

"It isn't impossible. King, do you have photographs of any of these characters?"

"Yes, sir, the Jardine brothers and Jug and Steamroller and I think there's a distant shot of The Weight."

"Good. Duplicate them and have them distributed to the uniformed branch. McCusker will be keeping his head down. By now he knows that we know he killed Bill McGarrigle, and he's wanted for police assault, but the others might venture into the bars. I also want you to lend yourself to the hunt, Montgomerie." Montgomerie nodded.

"If we can't collar them by tomorrow

176

evening we'll alert the bank and wait for them there."

"Do we draw firearms, sir?" Montgomerie sucked fiercely before speaking.

"Not yet." Donoghue took his pipe out of his mouth and laid it on one side while he wrote on his notepad. He tore the page off and handed it to King. "I want you to call on this address and speak to a woman called Samantha Simonds. She lived there five years ago, she may well still be there. Talk to her about her flatmate of five years ago, Anne McDonald."

"Samantha Simonds." King looked at the piece of notepaper. "That I suppose is the SS in Bill McGarrigle's abbreviated notes. Do you want me to look for any involvement on Spicer's part?"

"Good man." Donoghue smiled. "But be discreet. Ray and I are going to Dunlane. We'll meet back here at—" he glanced at his watch—"say six p.m. Montgomerie, you stay out on the street. Don't report in unless you have any concrete information about the whereabouts of McCusker and his pals."

"Very good, sir."

"Wherever do they get their names from, Jug . . ."

"Haven't a clue, sir."

"No, I expect you haven't. Oh, and Montgomerie . . ."

"Sir?"

"Try and stay off the booze during working hours. It'll help your thought process."

Sussock declined Donoghue's invitation to join him at the Burger bar for a snack. He went to the small room with tables and chairs and a cooker and fridge which was optimistically referred to as the "canteen", and began to forage for food. Eventually he had three slices of nearly stale bread, a chunk of very stale cheese and a tin of beans, the dust on which indicated that it might have been resting in the corner of the bottom cupboard since the day "P" Division station was built in 1927. He hustled himself beans on toast and grated the cheese over the meal. He cleared his plate ravenously and then set about hunting for the ingredients of a cup of tea. Nobody had left any teabags lying around but someone had been careless enough to leave a jar of instant coffee on top of the refrigerator—good stuff too. Sussock carried the steaming mug of coffee up to the CID rooms and drank it while reading King's Sunday paper. The meal would see him through until evening because he was nothing if not a survivor. He drained his mug and went down to the car park at the rear of the building to meet Donoghue.

HM Prison Dunlane began life in the late eighteenth century as the country home of a newly rich Glasgow tobacco merchant. It was built in the low rolling hills of southern Lanarkshire and had passed through a succession of owners before coming into the possession of the Scottish Office. It then became an open prison which, with ingenious use of outhouses, gatehouses and prefabricated "temporary" buildings, housed seventy-three prisoners, staff and the families of staff. Fabian Donoghue turned his Rover through the tall stone gateposts and put the car at the long driveway, threequarters of an hour after leaving central Glasgow.

He pulled the car smoothly to a stop outside the main door of the old house. The prison officer on duty at the door inspected their I/D's and escorted them to the administration block where they were received by Deputy Governor Brewer.

"I'm sorry to arrive with only a 'phone call as notice, Mr. Brewer." Donoghue and Brewer shook hands. Donoghue glanced out of the window on to a lawn at the rear of the building on which a football match was being played, with all players stripped to the waist.

"The Scottish obsession with football is a mystery to me," said Brewer. "They'll grab any chance of a game, even on a day like this." He shook hands with Sussock.

"Can't see how they can tell one side from the other." Donoghue smiled.

"Please, take a seat gentlemen."

Brewer was a young man, hardly in his thirties, he was tall and well built, and seemed to Donoghue to have an odd mixture of military manner and small boy charm. Behind Brewer's desk, on the bookcase, was a picture of a squad of RAF personnel in dress uniform, drawn up in front of a fighter aircraft. Donoghue surmised that Brewer had recently joined the Prison Service from a commission in the RAF, but never having been in the Armed Services, could tell nothing else. Ray Sussock, though, had done his national service in the RAF just after the last war, he'd seen the world as far as Cornwall and had risen to the rank of corporal in the RAF Regiment. He immediately identified Brewer as a pain in the arse chinless wonder from the catering corps, who, despite the deadly-looking aircraft in the photograph, had probably piloted nothing more than the squadron jeep.

"Coffee, gentlemen?" asked Brewer.

"Thank you," said Donoghue. Sussock grunted.

Brewer picked up the 'phone on his desk and requested a pot of coffee. Replacing the receiver, he asked how he could help, addressing only Donoghue.

"It concerns a prisoner known as Jack Gilheaney, also known as 'Granite' Gilheaney."

"Ah," said Brewer.

"You know him?"

"Oh yes, quite well. He's on my wing and I'm in the process of collating all his reports. He's applied for parole and his application will be heard at next week's parole board."

"Bit early in the piece for parole, isn't it?" asked Donoghue.

181

"Much too early. He's only just transferred in from Peterhead, less than twelve months ago, and he was very lucky to get an open prison so early in his sentence. He committed a particularly brutal murder, as I imagine you know. However, he's now entitled to apply and so his appeal will be heard."

"How do you rate his chances?"

"Nil." Brewer stood and took a file out of the cabinet which stood next to his desk. "Like I said, it's too early in the overall sentence of fifteen years and it's also too early in his stay here. We haven't really assessed his suitability for a less structured environment, such as ours."

"How was he transferred from Peterhead?" asked Sussock.

Brewer looked at Sussock with a puzzled expression, and then said, "Oh, I see, why was he transferred? I'm new to Scotland and some of the expressions are still strange, but my wife's picking it up rapidly. She's already going for her messages instead of doing the shopping. Well, why was he transferred? He's been in and out of institutions all his life; he was no discipline problem in Peterhead; he's getting on—at

182

forty-two he's a very old lag, most prisoners are in their twenties and thirties—and he was regarded as a burned-up recidivist, that's how his Senior Hall Officer at Peterhead described him in the transfer report." Brewer leafed through the file, "Yes, here it is: 'Gilheaney is a burned-up recidivist. He has no place in a top security gaol as a category A prisoner,' unquote. So with that and the fact that Peterhead is bursting at the seams, they transferred him here. But we've got a lot of work to do with him before he's ready for parole."

"What work?" asked Donoghue.

There was a tap on the door. A warder entered the office with a tray of coffee and biscuits which he laid on the table. He then left the room quietly.

"Well, he's very institutionalized. He's spent most of his life inside: grew up in an orphanage, been inside mental hospitals and prisons, never had a job to speak of, criminal convictions for violent crime of an impetuous nature. His last offence, the murder of that girl, is the only offence which suggested premeditation. He apparently ambushed her near her home; he must have found out her address and planned it very thoroughly. Generally though, his acts of violence seemed to arise out of frustration, so what we are doing here is gradually giving him more freedom so he can develop tolerance and self-discipline."

"Are you getting anywhere?"

"Too early to tell yet, but he's not given us cause for concern so far."

"What does he say about the crime, his last?"

"Maintains his innocence, which by the way is another reason why he won't get parole. Acceptance of guilt is a prerequisite of parole. He still clings to that cock-and-bull story he made up when arrested."

"That he went to meet his solicitor?" said Sussock.

"That's right," said Brewer. "Do you know the case?"

"I arrested him."

"Oh really. Apparently he fought all the way." Brewer turned the pages of Gilheaney's file.

"Yes. Never changed his story despite the reaction it got in the High Court."

"Which was?"

"Open laughter. It didn't faze him at all

and he repeated it a few months later in the Court of Criminal Appeal in Edinburgh."

"It doesn't surprise me," said Brewer. "He's clung to the same story despite derision from other inmates." He leaned forward and began to pour the coffee. "But other than that he hasn't used any direct action to draw attention to his professed innocence. No rooftop demonstrations, no hunger strikes; he's too tame, too unimaginative. His biggest problem is choosing recreational pursuits instead of being told what to do."

"How bright is he?" Donoghue reached for a cup of coffee.

"Well, here's the psychologist's report." Brewer handed Donoghue a sheet of paper. "You'll see that he seems to be down to earth, he doesn't have any flights of fancy or any tendency to withdraw into himself. He did well on the dictation test, writing it all down, joining letters and separating words, a few spelling mistakes but that's nothing to worry about. I think it says there that he can read an article in a tabloid newspaper and show an understanding of it in a brief discussion. He knew the date and the name of the Prime Minister."

"The psychologist notes no evidence of emotional or psychological disturbance, but below average intelligence." Donoghue handed the report to Sussock.

"I think that's a trifle unfair," said Brewer. "Do help yourself to biscuits, gentlemen. You see, it doesn't allow for an acute inferiority complex which doesn't permit Gilheaney to exercise his full potential. I've spoken to him and observed him with other inmates, and occasionally there's a spark, a sudden release of intellectual energy so to speak, then he gets overawed and retreats back into his usual flat self. It doesn't surprise me that the psychologist dismisses him like that, I've yet to meet a psychologist who possesses a real degree of insight. However, for Gilheaney, it's too late. He'll never be able to overcome a lifetime in institutions."

"What is his history?"

"Brought up in a gigantic children's home near Aberdeen, army, a bit of an itinerant according to his form. Listen to this. Wolverhampton Magistrates: three months for assault. Newcastle Assize—that dates him—two years for GBH. Then he was detained under the Mental Health Act in a hospital in Greater London. He was there for three years and that, I think, did most of the damage."

"Why?" asked Donoghue.

"Well, simply because institutional life in a mental hospital is soporific. They sit in their pyjamas all day drugged up to the eyeballs with only token therapy. The army and prison are institutions, but the regime is vigorous and there's the guarantee of freedom to cling to, at least for most of them. There's no such guarantee in mental hospitals; you're in and drugged up until the administration lets you out."

Donoghue nodded.

"Well, after he was discharged from the hospital he worked his way west. Reading Magistrates: one month for drunken behaviour. Swindon Magistrates: one month drunk and disorderly. Cardiff Crown Court—by the time he got to Wales the Assizes had been replaced by the Crown Courts and the one at Cardiff sent him down for a couple of years for assaulting a police officer."

"I get the picture," said Donoghue.

"Depressing, isn't it?" replied Brewer. "The gist of the rest is that he makes his way north over a period of four years with only small stretches inside, finally ending up in Glasgow five years ago facing a charge of murder. He was all of thirty-seven at the time."

"And he's been here for one year?"

"Almost twelve months, yes. His Senior Hall Officer says that Gilheaney gets on with the other inmates; he's accepted rather than been part of the in crowd, which is basically the football team." Brewer nodded towards the window. "The other inmates also give him a certain amount of respect because of his age. The chaplain has hardly seen him, which is unusual because most of the inmates who are coming up for parole tend to be regular attenders at chapel, Bible class and the Alcoholics Anonymous group."

"But not Gilheaney?"

"No. His supervisor at the workshop says that he's a steady hand, gets on with his job and doesn't idle about or talk too much. He works in the tailor's shop, on the pressing machine. Actually it's one of our more responsible jobs."

"A model prisoner."

"It's going to be one of the best parole reports in a long time when I've assembled it all," said Brewer. "He won't get it, though, for the reasons I've given; also because prisoners tend not to get parole at their first application as a matter of policy, but mainly he won't get it because of the police report, from your office no doubt."

"Who sent it in?"

Brewer looked at the bottom of the report. "It's signed by a Chief Superintendent Findlater. He says that the crime was a brutal assault, the girl was stabbed a number of times in the chest and she was also strangled. He goes on to say that it was a premeditated attack and the experienced investigating officer described it as one of the worst he'd ever seen."

"Did you say that, Ray?" asked Donoghue.

"I can't honestly remember, sir."

"Would it be possible to interview Gilheaney?" Donoghue sipped his coffee.

"Certainly," replied Brewer, and picked up his 'phone.

"I don't think it would be wise for you to be present, Ray," Donoghue said, turning to Sussock. "I'll see him alone."

Donoghue was startled to see how small Gilheaney was. He stood at the entrance to the agent's room, holding his hands crossed in front of him, looking blankly at Donoghue, slight and thinly built, probably a few inches over five feet tall.

"Come in and sit down," said Donoghue, and then added, "please".

Gilheaney shuffled in and sat on the chair at the other side of the table. The agents' rooms were housed in what was once the grooms' quarters above the stables of the old house; they were cramped and dim. The only decoration was a NO SMOKING sign in rigid black letters.

Donoghue introduced himself. He asked about the food and he and Gilheaney chatted about the conditions in comparison to Peterhead. When he thought Gilheaney was relaxed he said, "You're in here for murder. Will you tell me what happened?"

"I don't know what happened. I didn't do it."

"How long had you been in Glasgow before you were arrested?"

"About a month. That's about how long I can last without causing trouble for somebody."

"Where were you staying?"

"Guest-house on Great Western Road. I can't remember the name."

"You can remember the name of the road," said Donoghue.

"It sticks in my mind. It's a name which sounds like it's got somewhere to go."

"So how did you cause trouble?"

"Och, it was nothing. I had a bottle of wine and I was singing in George Square. I wasn't out to do anybody any harm but I was making a noise right enough."

"You were arrested?"

"Aye, but I wasn't kept in. I was charged with Breach of the Peace and summonsed to appear before the Sheriff. I got a week's notice, like, so I went and saw a solicitor. It was summertime and I don't like being inside when the weather's good. I was hoping to get off with a fine. Without a solicitor I thought the Sheriff would jack me back inside so I went to the first solicitor's I saw."

"Which was?"

"I don't remember all the names but the one I saw was called Spicer. He had a funny wee arm."

"Go on."

"Well, I saw him and he took all my particulars."

"You mean your history and details of the charge."

"Aye, and where I was staying."

"How long were you with him?"

"Long time."

"Hour?"

"Two more like. It was one of the best services I've ever had. He was really getting to know me. Most of them, they just have you in for ⟨…⟩ ⟨…⟩ ⟨…⟩ and they don't really listen. There ⟨…⟩ one guy in England, he got my details m⟨…⟩d up with another guy's, started telling ⟨…⟩ beaks all about my children. Me, I never even had a girl-friend, except one girl in Catterick but that was a long time ago, she . . ."

"Let's stick with Glasgow," said Donoghue. "What happened then?"

"See, well I gone over this in my head so many times I'm not sure I'm not mixedup."

Donoghue grunted involuntarily. He felt Gilheaney's statement to be disarmingly honest. "Tell me what you think happened."

"Well, Mr. Spicer gave me another appointment for a couple of days after I first saw him. He said it was to go over my plea with him and just check on a few details, something like that. He wrote it on a little card and gave it to me. When I went back to keep the appointment his secretary said he was busy and seeing no one. She was rude, really rude, saying bad things to me."

"Such as?"

"Said something about Mr. Spicer couldn't be bothered with filth like me, called me rotten and scum, words like that. I know I done bad thi‍ out a young lassie shouldn't say thing that."

"What happened ther

"I showed her the car with the date and time on it. It was a bit screwed up having been in my pocket but you could read it all right. Anyway she snatched it and tore it up and told me to get out because I was making the place stink." He fell silent.

"Then what?"

"I started to shout, sir. I know I shouldn't have done it, I know I should have fallen in with the routine but I didn't want to go inside in the summertime."

"What did you shout?"

"I said I'd batter her. I said if she went on like that I'd swing for her." He swallowed.

"Then she started screaming, really screaming, at me. The people in the other room, the outside waiting-room came in and heard me. Also Mr. Spicer came out of his office. The girl was pointing at me and said, 'That thing threatened me.' I remember that. I started to talk to Mr. Spicer but he yelled at me to get out. So I left."

"Then . . ." nudged Donoghue.

"Next day at the guest-house, early, about eight, you have to be out by nine, the woman who runs the place tells me my brother's on the 'phone for me and shouts at me for having personal calls. She was away before I could tell her I didn't have no brother. Well, when I gets on the 'phone it was Mr. Spicer. He says he has to meet me to discuss my case and asks if I knew where the Botanical Gardens were. I said I did, so he tells me to meet him in this lane behind the gardens at eleven o'clock that night. He told me how to get to it, it was opposite a garage."

"Didn't you think that was a strange thing to request?"

"Aye, so I did, but when somebody like your solicitor tells you to do something you do it, 'less you want deeper trouble, and I didn't want to go inside in the summer."

"So you went?"

"Aye. It was a Fair Friday night. That didn't mean much to me but the whole city seemed to be drunk. I had some money and I had a bit of whisky in me."

"Do you remember what happened?"

"I think so." Gilheaney paused for a moment. "Well, it was light, you know how in Scotland it stays light really late in the summertime?"

Donoghue nodded.

"Well, it was like that, late, but I could see a long way, it was really warm and the plants in the gardens were smelling very strong. I remember the evening well, it was the last time I was a free man. I found the lane and stood at the entrance. A few cars went by but I didn't see Mr. Spicer so I walked down the lane and I saw these legs."

"Legs?"

"Woman's legs, sticking out of the bushes. So I went over, she was lying on her front, I turned her over and she was all bloody with a knife sticking out of her middle, so I pulled it out and ran to get some help. I didn't run far because a police van pulled up at the side of me."

"Mmm." Donoghue nodded slowly. He had read the file on the murder and asked "I understand there was some question of you being in possession of the girl' belongings?"

"You mean the keyring?"

Donoghue grunted.

"Mr. Spicer gave them to me. In that long session I had with him, at the end he said he was clearing out some drawers and did have use for a purse. So I said aye, it gave me somewhere to keep my money. So he gave it to me. It was a small purse and keyring combined."

"Did you keep the keys?"

"Yes, I left them on. It made me fee important to have keys in my pocket."

"It didn't occur to you that it was a strange thing for a solicitor to do, give a client a purse with a bunch of keys attached to them?"

"No. He told me the reason."

In the car returning to Glasgow Donoghue did not talk to Sussock, he wa pondering on the case for the prosecution against Jack "the Granite" Gilheaney alleged perpetrator of the notorious Fair Friday murder. Indicated at the instance of Her Majesty's Advocate, defendant is a man with a long criminal history with previous convictions for violence. Defendant was heard to threaten the life of the deceased the day prior to the murder. Defendant was apprehended fleeing the scene of the crime still in possession of the murder weapon. Defendant was found to be in possession of victim's purse containing x pounds and y pence, and was also found to be in possession of victim's house keys.

The long bungalow which stood in solitary splendour was in fact called the Bar J but otherwise it was as King described it. A white gate and then a drive which hooked around a pond, finishing in an open area in front of the house. The bungalow was the same colour as the gate, pure virgin white, uncomfortably clinical. An off-white or a cream colour which hinted at a degree of self knowledge would have put Montgomerie more at ease. He was disturbed by Tiny Jardine's choice of colour for his house, he felt it a bit like Gipsy Rose Lee shuffling along the aisle in a stiff white gown, blushing behind a posy of flowers. He was also disturbed because he didn't know what he was doing, standing there in front of the door. Nobody had told him to interview Tiny Jardine, nobody knew where he was, he did not know what he was going to say. He should at that moment be in the West End checking out the bars for Jug and Steamroller. He decided to ring the bell once, just once, and then leave if nobody heard it. He pressed the button, which to his dismay resulted in a long peel of bells which chimed through the house, and set at least three dogs barking. The door was opened by a tough-looking bruiser who Montgomerie felt was used to remaining vertical after punch-ups. He looked down at Montgomerie, amused, curious, as to the identity of the person who had the affrontery to drive up to the front door and set the dogs off.

"Police," said Montgomerie. He flashed his I/D.

The man's face hardened. His eyes got cold, he pulled his shoulders back and looked like a villain.

"I'd like to talk to Tiny," said Montgomerie, looking up at the thing holding the door with fleshy paws. Nicotined-stained, too, noted Montgomerie.

"What about?" The man spoke slowly.

"That's between me and him."

"I'll have to check with the boss," said the man. He laboured each word but Montgomerie had the impression he was talking as fast as possible.

"Go check," said Montgomerie. "I'll wait here."

"You wait here," said the man. "I'll go check." He shut the door behind him.

Montgomerie looked around him. The lawn was vast and neatly tended, cut close, but sprouting daisies here and there. The pond had water-lilies floating and the whole spread was fenced off with parallel planks running between posts. He turned his gaze back to the house. At either side of the door stood two little figures of cowboys, about two feet high, cast in plaster and brightly painted. Montgomerie reached down and grabbed the sand-coloured Stetson of one of the figures and tipped it backwards. A door key was lying under the base of the figure.

"Cowpoke never knows what he's a sittin' on," drawled Montgomerie.

The man lumbered back to the front door and pulled it wide. "Boss says you can come in," said the man. "He's resting, says you have to join him for a beer."

He led Montgomerie through the house. The floor was wood, the walls were plaster, prints of the old West hung everywhere.

"My name's Tex," said the man.

"Had to be," murmured Montgomerie. "The boss give you that handle, or is it original?"

"The boss," said Tex, descending a short flight of stairs, a manoeuvre in which he found difficulty retaining his balance, not unlike, thought Montgomerie, a grizzly bear in the Grand Tetons. Montgomerie also took each step with care, to ease the pain in his ribs. "Boss likes cowboys and that, my real name's Stephen, I used to stay in Drumchapel. I used to hang around with the Mad Spaniard till he was filled in one night. You're lucky, the boss is in a good mood today."

"He gets bad moods?" asked Montgomerie, glancing at the print of Remington's *"Battle for the Waterhole"* as he walked by it.

"Oh, yeah. When the boss is in a bad

mood he just grabs the nearest thing to him and chucks it. Last week he threw one of the girls through the window."

The corridor opened out into a lounge. There were chairs and settees in an old-fashioned design with the backs held to the sides with cords, an open hearth in which lay the remains of a small wood fire; a pair of horns from a bull were pinned to the wall and there were guns arranged in a rack. The walls were of brick painted over. Two girls were in the room, dressed in cowgirl outfits, short leather mini skirts, waistcoats, boots and Stetsons tipped back on their heads, smiling transparently. Tiny Jardine sat on one of the settees, holding a glass of beer in his hands. He was dressed in a housecoat and was probably a little taller than he was wide. When Montgomerie came into the room Tiny Jardine smiled like a hungry cougar sizing up a foal.

"This is the boss," said Tex. "Boss, this is the polis."

"Hi, pardner," said Tiny. "Sorry I ain't dressed proper but I just come in from the pool." As he said it the sound of a splash followed by female laughter echoed down one of the corridors leading off the lounge.

"Oh, I quite understand," said Montgomerie, suddenly feeling very British, like he found he did when on package holidays. "I'm sorry I called unexpectedly."

"I wasn't busy." Tiny continued to smile. "Susie, go fix our guest a drink."

"I . . ." began Montgomerie but was silenced by Tiny's teeth.

"No man comes in my house and doesn't get a drink, pardner."

Susie stood, looking like a young Scottish lassie acting out a rich man's fantasies, and looking as though the only range she had been near was the one in the kitchen. She walked with a sexy walk through some hanging beads and down a corridor marked "Saloon". Another corridor was marked "Chuck Wagon". The corridor which led to the swimming pool wasn't marked at all, but then that led to the twentieth century, heated, chlorinated water, and sunbeds.

"Some place you have here," said Montgomerie.

"Built it myself."

"With your own two hands?" said Montgomerie, pouring ice on to the situation. "Or do you mean it was built to your specifications by an army of coolies?"

"Now, son . . ." Tiny still smiled but no longer with enthusiasm. Montgomerie let it rest there. He wanted a dialogue, but he didn't want to be Tiny's best buddie, especially after knowing him for all of sixty seconds. "Been here long?" he asked.

"Here's your beer," said Tiny as Susie wriggled through the beads, holding a tray containing a glass of lager. "Take the weight off your feet, pardner." Then Tiny smiled again, just to let Montgomerie know he wasn't inviting him to do anything.

Montgomerie sank into the settee, which he found lower and more comfortable than he'd imagined. He took the lager from the tray and sipped it. It was served chilled, American style.

"Those real?" he asked, nodding to the collection of rifles and revolvers on the wall.

"Imitations, pardner," said Tiny, watching Susie walk past him on her way back to the Saloon. The other girl also left the room with Susie, silently and without fuss: leaving the men to talk men talk. Tiny turned back to Montgomerie. "The irons are real, though."

"Irons?"

"By the fire. Branding irons. I brought them back from a trip I made a few years ago. Belonged to a ranch called the Split R."

Montgomerie twisted in his seat and saw the irons: long metal bars lying in front of hearth. He had seen them as he came into the room and in his naivety in such matters had assumed them to be two common or garden very British pokers. He sipped his lager and smiled, turning back to face Tiny.

"What can I do for you, pardner?" smiled Tiny Jardine. "What brought you here?"

"I don't honestly know," said Montgomerie truthfully, and feeling that he wanted to be a million miles away.

"Well, pardner, that means we have a problem. I like entertaining but my home isn't exactly open to the public."

"Well . . ." Montgomerie felt his throat constrict.

"Take your time, pardner." Tiny Jardine's teeth flashed. He drank from his glass. "Take some beer, you want some more beer?"

Montgomerie shook his head. It was rapidly and crushingly dawning on him that walking up to Tiny's front door wasn't exactly the most sensible thing he had done in his career, which itself hadn't been exactly unchequered. If there was one thing he had excelled at, it was getting himself into a mess, frequently, and the only thing he now expected to get out of this, his latest act of impetuosity, was his P45 with his next pay advice. He drank some more lager and didn't feel himself the biggest, most sensible police officer in the West of Scotland.

"See, pardner," said Tiny, "I reckon you got to be here for a reason, so it's either official or criminal, 'cos it certainly isn't going to be personal. I don't have dicks in my address book. You're not asking any questions so I guess it's one thing. You sure have a brass neck though, I usually have to make the first approach. Anyway, what is it, mortgage round your neck, woman trouble? How much do you want? Think of a number and halve it and then tell me what I get in return."

Montgomerie choked on his lager.

"Take it easy, son. It's hard the first time. You're straight CID, aren't you, not in the Drug Squad? No? Pity."

"I'm not on the take, Jardine."

Montgomerie stood, hissing like a cornered cat, but he knew the screw was already in and turning.

"Sure you're not, son." Tiny Jardine smiled.

Montgomerie threw his glass away to his side. It smashed against the gun rack. "I'm investigating a murder," he snarled. "You're implicated, Jardine."

"Oh aye? So how do you work that one out, pardner?"

"We've traced the link," Montgomerie was still shaking with rage. "From Neutron John McCusker to Spicer to you."

"Is that right, son?" Tiny Jardine remained seated and looked up at Montgomerie. "That is interesting. A guy called Spicer, you say?"

"Don't come that with me, Jardine. I'm going to nail you."

"Yes, yes. I realize we have to say that. Shall we say a hundred quid a week as a retainer?"

Leaving Tiny Jardine's house was something that Montgomerie could never recall accurately. He just had a disjointed, dreamlike memory of crashing from side to side down the corridor, flinging a door open, with a deep belly laugh resounding behind him.

In the car his legs were jelly and his grip weak. He stopped at the verge and walked up the road for a mile before returning to the car. He leaned forward and rested his forehead on the steering-wheel. The least damaging thing he had just done had been to wreck the entire investigation. A passing motorist would think he was consulting a road map, or maybe suffering a little from car sickness.

King went to the address which Donoghue had given him. It was a basement flat in Clousten Street, G20. Samantha Simonds still lived there. He pressed the bell.

"I didn't care for her much, Mr. King," said Ms Simonds. "I have my girl-friends, you understand, but snotty little Annie wasn't one of them. She liked the boys. The bigger the car the better she liked them. 'Boys', I say. Darling, some of them were, as they say, old enough to be her daddy."

Samantha Simonds was a short stocky woman who King guessed to be about forty-five. She had walked in front of him down the long corridor to the sitting-room where two women were sitting on the floor sewing. Samantha Simonds clapped her hands and said "Shoo" as she entered the room and the two women immediately left. She sat in a leather armchair and reached for a heavy briar pipe. She smoked it, looking intently at King, daring him to smirk.

"Snotty?" said King.

"As snotty as hell," growled the woman, pulling strongly on the pipe. "She must have thought her double-barrelled name and private education counted for something. Well, it didn't cut any ice in here, not while I was around."

"Double-barrelled?"

"Forbes-McDonald. Miss Anne Forbes-McDonald from Edinburgh, if you please," said Samantha Simonds in a mock Morningside accent, which King had to admit wasn't a bad stab and which suggested that Samantha Simonds wasn't wholly gin-alley raised herself. "Educated in a private day school because Daddy didn't agree with boarding but doesn't like the state system. Daddy, you understand, is a banker. Not any banker, you understand, but a senior manager in the Bank of Scotland."

"I see," said King. "I gather you two didn't hit it off?"

"I hated the posh little calculating cow."

"Why?"

"Oh, don't ask stupid bloody questions. I just did."

"I take it that you don't own this pad?"

"I don't, dammit. If I did Anne bloody what's-her-name wouldn't have got her face in here."

"Figures," said King.

"What do you mean by that, cop?"

"Simply that your hostility is apparent," said King, trying to cool a rapidly heating situation. "Do you think the feeling was mutual?"

"Probably. The cow hated anybody who was for the people."

"You're for the people?"

"Right. Superman is a myth. Power to the people. Join the people's crusade, comrade."

"No, thanks," said King. "I've got a job to do."

"Cops!" She struck a match and put it to her pipe even though the inferno already in the bowl didn't need any help.

"What did posh little Annie do for a living? How did she put bread on her table?"

"Worked for a solicitor. She didn't need to, that was obvious."

"How?"

"Well, she couldn't have afforded her lifestyle on her spending money salary. I mean her clothes, she practically bought out Fraser's each and every Saturday. So the extra money came from Daddy, had to, the senior manager in the Royal Bank, remember?" King nodded.

"Did you ever meet her employer?"

"Spicer was his name, can't forget that, thin face like a rat with a fixed grin and underdeveloped arm." She sucked on her pipe and blew out some grey bitter smelling smoke. "They didn't get on. He came here one night and they had a real set-to."

"When was that?"

"Christ's sake, I don't know. All this was five years ago."

"One year before she died, two days before?"

"Oh I see." She shrugged her shoulders. "A year, maybe more. Throughout that last year or eighteen months she went to work like she was going to war."

210

"What do you mean?"

"It was her manner, single-minded, gearing up for a fight, heavy footfall. She looked the part and I dare say her old man was something big in the Edinburgh banking houses, but the silly little cow reminded me of those poison dwarves who come up from Hawick or somewhere with big chips on their little shoulders. You know the type, don't know how to move and are full of prejudice."

"Why did she stay with Spicer?"

"You know the type as well as I do: only happy with a hostile relationship." Samantha Simonds tapped her pipe out on a big black ashtray. "You've seen it, the 'I'm going to be faultless at my job so's you can't give me the push' attitude, but me and my awesome psyche are going to ruin you and your little operation. She kind of fed on other people's positives like a bit of anti-matter."

"Anti-what?"

"You wouldn't understand."

"Try me."

"Anti-matter. It's a sci-fi concept, earthling. That which feeds on matter, consumes positives. She went to work each day spruced up and clean as a new pin, bent on the continuing destruction of Spicer's little empire. This was five years ago, see how she still infests my life."

"Odd girl," said King.

"Odd! She had a cleanliness fetish, she used to accuse me of cooking chips only to ruin her sheets which were hanging drying in the kitchen. When she'd finished in the bathroom you'd have to take a spanner to the taps, she'd screwed them down so tight. Ugh!"

"Do you think she was effective with Spicer?"

"Yes, very. He came here like I said and they fought Guadalcanal over again. Bloody vicious it was—I loved it."

"What were they saying?"

"Difficult to remember and I didn't hear that much. These walls are very thick. But one thing sticks, he called her a criminal and she laughed and said that that was rich coming from him."

"So they disliked each other?"

"Right to the end. Now you mention it, I do remember that she lost her house key just before that Fair Friday night when that clochard did the citizens of Big G a favour. She had to wait for me to come home before she could get in. I was late one night, having been bending my elbow with some of the chaps from work—I teach, crime hound—so Miss Anne Forbes-McDonald had to kick her heels longer than usual. She'd been kicking them in some bar apparently, because when I came home she was sitting on the stairs pretty steamboats, I mean half cut. Anyway she said something about having 'got' him, and was 'screwing him stupid'. I remember that."

"Screwing?"

"Not sexually. All her men paid and paid but the ones she wore were made of galvanized steel. So why all this sudden interest in fair Anne of Morningside? You're the second this week."

"Who was the first?"

"That reporter. Wanted to see her things. I was to meet him later on Rutherglen Main Street to talk about Anne bloody Forbes-McDonald, but I never made it, the car wouldn't start. I read in the paper how he was attacked. Sad that, he was a nice old boy, had a kind of juvenile excitement about him, as though he was a Catholic and had actually listened when the priest had told him never to lose that sense of childish wonder."

"Priest said that to you, did he?"

"Once. I won't tell you what I said in reply but I hear he's still lighting candles and praying for me."

"You still have her things here, then?"

"Some. All her clothes and some papers. Nobody's ever collected them, earth cop, and I am humble and honest, so I haven't chucked them. I got the factor to let me take over the full tenancy so I can sub-let to my friends. Felicity uses snotty Annie's clothes, they fit very well. We see it as creative storage."

"I bet you do. Can I see her room?"

King was shown a small bedroom which smelled of lavender and had a poster of a horse on the wall and some cuddly toys on the pillow.

"This is sweet little Felicity's room," said Samantha Simonds, who was standing close enough to King for him to catch whisky as well as strong tobacco on her breath. "Annie's things are in the corner."

In the corner were half a dozen boxes stacked in a pile. All seemed to contain her papers, or books.

"Clothes?" asked King.

"Wardrobe," said Samantha Simonds. "Creative storage, as I said."

King grunted. He said he was taking the boxes of papers away.

"You can do that?" asked Samantha Simonds.

"Just watch me," said King, but eventually he succeeded in enlisting her help to carry the boxes to his car.

King emptied the contents of the boxes on to his desk in the CID rooms and sifted through them. He knew that Spicer had been through them before, five years before, looking for something on the pretext of helping the bereaved Carol, who was soon to become his wife, sort through her late sister's things. By the time King was able to sift through the boxes they mostly contained only press cuttings about the good life, expensive homes, exclusive resorts, fashion, men in the public eye, movie moguls, industrialists, top right-wing politicians. The pipedreams of a street kid. King worked with patience and care, examining each cutting, but found nothing of any relevance to Spicer or Gilheaney or the Jardine brothers.

He was disappointed. The sun was beating through the window and sweat was trickling off his forehead and over his fleshy cheeks. He went to the canteen to make himself some coffee, working on the theory that if you're hot the best way to cool down is to take a warm drink and heat up your inside, so reducing the heat differential. He reached for his jar of coffee from the top of the refrigerator and noticed that it had been plundered, but shrugged his shoulders and took what he needed, putting the jar back on top of the refrigerator. He carried his drink back up to the CID rooms. As he entered the office where he worked a draught blew one of the newspaper cuttings off his desk. As it floated over and over in the sun's rays King caught a glimpse of indentations on the paper. He picked it up and held it against the light. The indentations had been caused by a bold, old-fashioned typeface, as though the cutting, having been selected for its news content, had then been seen as a handy bit of paper to slip behind a sheet of typing paper to protect the typewriter roller. That it was still discernible after five years gave an indication of how the keys had been hammered. It was possible to read it in full:

One-armed Bandit.

How long did you think you'd get away with it? I cottoned on to you right from the start, I've photocopied your crooked accounts. You want me to go to the police? If you don't you'd better pay up. Otherwise I'll keep it shut for £50 per week to begin with.

Think it over, Spicer. I'll let you know who I am in a week or so. The money will be backdated to today's date anyhow.

King rummaged through the cuttings, holding each one up to the light. He found only two others which had been used as backing paper and he put them in obvious chronological order:

Spicer, Work late tonight. I'll be the only one left in the office typing pool by 7.00 p.m. We can talk business, maybe over dinner. They say the best thing to do when you're being blackmailed is to go to the law—why don't you? You could fix me up with at least two years suspended sentence for doing this. First offence, previous good character and all that. You of course would get at least five years.

217

You would also lose your livelihood and would have to sell your house and boat in order to repay all those poor punters who you have ripped off. I've only gone back eighteen months and already you have embezzled enough to buy a new Rolls-Royce. And what about poor Mr. McNulty (not so poor, though—hah!)—what will it do to him to have all this come out? Such a scandal and one of the most respected firms of solicitors in the city. But I don't think you're really interested in Mr. McNulty. Anyway see you at seven, blue eyes. Let's go somewhere good—after all, this is the beginning of a business partnership and since it's based on mutual distrust it should last quite a long time.

On a magazine cutting about the good life in Corfu was written:

Spicer, I saw the way you looked at me this morning. Don't try it, pal. Remember I've got evidence against you, it'll be found as soon as my parents come and collect my things. My father is in banking, remember, he reads accounts like you read the glossy magazines in your desk drawer.

King copied the letters down and included them in a report about his visit to Samantha Simonds's house. He had completed it ready for typing when Sussock and Donoghue arrived back from Dunlane Gaol. Sussock flopped in a chair and mopped his brow. Donoghue stood and read over King's report, grunting occasionally. He walked across the room and slipped King's report in the already overflowing basket which was marked "for typing". He told Sussock and King to sign out and get some rest; he told them they'd be working tomorrow.

Donoghue walked along the corridor to his office, sat at his desk and picked up the 'phone. He consulted a small notebook and then dialled an unlisted number.

"Can I talk to Dr. Reynolds?" he asked when a female voice answered.

Moments later a rich male voice said, "Reynolds."

"DI Donoghue, sir," said Donoghue. "I'm sorry to call at such an inconvenient time, but I feel it's urgent. It concerns a murder enquiry of five years ago, the so-called Fair Friday Murder."

"I remember the newspaper reports but I don't recall the post mortem. Did I perform it?"

"Yes, sir. I have a copy in front of me. I wonder if it's possible for us to go over the notes you made?"

"I dare say that that is very possible. Could you meet me at the Royal Infirmary in half an hour?"

"Certainly, certainly. Thank you, sir," said Donoghue. "It really is very good of you to come out at short notice for such a request."

"Just be on time, please," said Reynolds. "I'm performing a PM in three-quarters of an hour. I could give you about fifteen minutes. I don't wish to be rude, but it *is* a holiday." He hung up.

"Yes, sir," said Donoghue into the dead phone.

Donoghue was waiting in the car park as Reynolds drove up in his Volvo. He was wearing a short-sleeved shirt and as he approached Donoghue he smiled and commented on the weather. Donoghue followed the tall silver-haired pathologist down to the basement of the hospital and into the path lab. They walked between a row of seats on one side, a glass screen on the other. On the far side of the glass screen a body lay under a sheet on the marble slab and a mortuary assistant with greased-down hair was laying instruments on a trolley.

"He was washed on to the beach at Saltcoats this morning," said Reynolds as they walked. "Probably put a lot of trippers off their lunch."

"Drowned?" asked Donoghue.

"Probably. Some linear contusions though."

"Knife attack?"

"That sort of thing." He pushed open the door of his office. "All right, the famous or should I say infamous Fair Friday Murder." He ran his fingers over the labels on his filing cabinet drawers. "Five years ago, Fair Friday, that would be July. What was the lassie's name?" He yanked open a drawer.

"McDonald, Anne."

Reynolds pursed his lips and shook his head. "I didn't do it, Mr. Donoghue. No McDonald here," he said, walking his fingers over the spines of the files.

"Try Forbes-McDonald," said Donoghue.

"Fanshaw . . . Forbes-McDonald." He extracted a file and laid it on the table. "Female Caucasian, aged twenty-three. Apparent age twenty-five/seven."

"That's the one," grunted Donoghue.

"Tragic death," said Reynolds. "All the young ones are."

"Can we go over your notes, Doctor?" asked Donoghue.

He thought better of disillusioning Reynolds by telling him that in life this particular tragic death had been a vitriolic and twisted blackmailer.

"Surely. Well, it's all here in black and white. Multiple stab wounds to the stomach and chest, one pierced her heart at the aorta—that was instantly fatal. There was pin-point bruising around the throat and other individual bruises, some superficial abrasions to her back and back of her head. That's it. She was stabbed to death."

"What form do the stab wounds take, sir?"

"Well, according to my notes, there were seven in total, they penetrated three to four

222

inches on a vertical plane angling from right of anterior to left of posterior."

"I'm sorry," said Donoghue.

"Well, the blade of the knife was pushed in on the right-hand side of the front of the body at such an angle that if it had impaled the woman, had gone right through her, it would have emerged on the left-hand side of her back, as if she was attacked from behind by a right-handed person."

"Or a left-handed person standing directly in front of her," said Donoghue.

"Yes, indeed." Reynolds nodded. "That would be my guess, but guesses are one thing I'm not allowed to give in evidence."

"Were you questioned closely in court, sir?"

Reynolds turned to the file. "You'll get a transcript of the trial without difficulty, but according to my notes I was merely asked to give the cause of death, which was the stab wound which penetrated the cardiac cavity, and to identify the murder weapon."

"Which you were able to do?"

"Oh yes, easily, the knife I saw was a single-edge weapon which fitted the depth and width of the wounds. There was also the characteristic 'fish tailing' around the puncture which you get with single-edged knives."

"Were you cross-examined, sir?"

"Not according to my notes. I'm bound to have recorded being cross-examined because it's always an uncomfortable experience."

"The wounds on the neck, what are they?"

"Strangulation marks. One hand, left-hand, single bruise on the left of the windpipe close to the angle of the jaw caused by the assailant's left thumb, and three bruises on the right of the neck caused by fingers of the left hand. Only three because the little finger doesn't usually have enough pressure to bruise."

"So she was strangled by a left-handed person?"

"She was strangled by the left hand of her assailant, that is all I can say, but given the direction of the stab wounds I'd say it was a fair possibility the assailant was a left-hander."

"The strangulation didn't kill her, though?"

"No. The venous return wasn't blocked."

"Was she strangled before or after being stabbed?"

"I couldn't tell. The skin tissue will still bruise for a few minutes after the heart has stopped."

"So without committing yourself, she could have been attacked by a left-handed person?"

"Yes."

"Using his right hand to restrain her while his left was doing all the damage?"

"Yes."

"Could he have had only one hand, his left, and still have perpetrated this attack?"

"Yes, but it's difficult to see how."

"Supposing he throttled her, to near or absolute unconsciousness, which would also have stopped her screaming, and then as she slumped to the ground he finished her off with his knife. Is that possible?"

"Of course," said Reynolds. "It's perfectly feasible. You don't need a pathologist to tell you that."

Donoghue walked across the baking heart of the bitch city. The inquiry was disturbing him but felt he was making progress. He felt he wasn't driving in the dark any more.

It was Fair Sunday 6.00 p.m.

9

MONTGOMERIE sat in the window of the upstairs bar sipping a lager and looking down on to Byres Road. It was a hot, hot day and the girls were in their summer clothes, he was young and handsome, he was healthy, the lager was good, the inside of the bar was cool, with not too many punters around.

He felt like a dog.

It hadn't got easier as Sunday had dragged towards Monday, walking round the West End, checking bars, hanging around on street corners, strolling through the park and the Botanical Gardens looking for Jardine's heavies and not seeing any. It was just the monotony of one foot in front of the other, that and no action, that had let it play on his mind until the guilt began to crush him, lowering his eyes to the ground, rounding his shoulders. He'd forced himself to walk in the heat up and down and down and up Byres Road until it was opening time and, like all problem cases, he'd sought refuge in booze. The fact that he had wrecked the investigation and his career was curiously easier to cope with than his sheer incredulity that he had driven up and knocked on Tiny Jardine's door in the first place. He was on his second lager when he saw Jug and Steamroller get out of a white Bentley. He got to the street as the Bentley was being driven away by Phil Jardine. Jug and Steamroller were standing on the street, they wore beards, had huge beer guts, they were roughly the size of a house and moved like tanks. The two men talked for a few minutes before Steamroller turned and lumbered off toward Partick. Jug hung around: so did Montgomerie.

Montgomerie crossed the road and stepped into a close, out of the heat, but still managed to keep an eye on Jug who was hovering near a bus stop. Eventually he hailed an inner circle bus. Montgomerie broke cover and jumped on the bus as Jug was squeezing his way up the stairs. Montgomerie flashed his transcard and sat downstairs. He left the bus at the city centre as it was about to start its fourth circumnavigation. He walked down

Sauchiehall Street and found Ray Sussock in the canteen.

"Heavy stuff," said Montgomerie when Sussock told him about the trip he and Donoghue had made to Dunlane Open Prison.

"It's not cut and dried yet, but damn near it. There's enough to question Gilheaney's guilt, that's for sure." There was a fine edge to Sussock's voice, like a blade that's so sharp you don't realize it's cut until a thin line seeps red over everything. "Five years is a big chunk to take out of anybody's life, Mal. There's no excuse, I should've dug deeper, but the surface of the case was so glossy I didn't want to spoil it. I didn't just need a murder conviction, I *needed* one. Five years ago I was in a big mess at home, all at sea here, I needed a feather in my cap."

"I reckon anybody would have done the same, Sarge, really."

Montgomerie sipped his coffee, holding the big white mug with both hands. "I mean, the mighty Fabian didn't start sniffing until a dying hack shoved Spicer's scent under his nose."

"Aye," said Sussock distantly, an over-the-mountain voice.

"It was found proven in the High Court and at Court of Criminal Appeal. You can't get higher than that. Anyway the PF prosecuted, not us, so you convinced those eejits."

"Aye," said Sussock.

"I didn't do too well either." Montgomerie had the urge to tell about his visit to Tiny Jardine's, to get it off his chest, to come clean. He balked. "I saw Jug and Steamroller dropped off by Phil Jardine—he drives a white Bentley. Anyway I went down into the street and was lamped straight away. Followed Jug, who took me on a ride on the inner circle. I was getting dizzy so I came here."

"You haven't blown the surveillance?"

"No," said Montgomery and felt a claw reach up from his gut and grab his heart. "No, they acted like they always do. Dick King's been watching them for weeks so there's no reason to assume that they know we're on to the Tuesday job."

No, he thought, no reason, there's still no reason.

"Hope you're right. What are your movements for the rest of the day?"

"I'm going to put a call through to

Rothesay, grab a bite to eat and get back up the West End for the evening. What are you doing for feeding time, Sarge?"

"Committing suicide," said Sussock.

King stood in front of the door and pressed the bell again. He waited in the cool dark stairway and was about to turn away when he heard a noise from inside the flat. The door opened. The new widow had aged, she was pale, she had furrows on her brow, her cheeks were hollow. She clutched her house robe to her throat and looked up at King with thinly watered, pleading eyes.

"I'm sorry to disturb you, Mrs. McGarrigle. I need to take another look in your late husband's study."

She made a high-pitched croaking noise and moved aside. King stepped over the threshold, the air was musty, the flat was dim, the two suitcases still stood packed and waited to be taken to Rimini. King went into the study. Mrs. McGarrigle shut the door and shuffled down the hall towards the sitting-room. King doubted that she recognized him.

He sat in the dead man's chair. He was there out of personal curiosity as much as for professional purposes and began to sift delicately through the mass of papers. Finally he found what he was looking for. It was a photocopy of a letter Gilheaney had sent to the *Clarion* from the slammer. The letter was short and to the point; writing in a clumsy labouring hand, Gilheaney was protesting his innocence and was asking the newspaper for help to prove that his brief had set him up. King guessed that the *Clarion* probably received many similar letters each year, and most certainly after each sitting of the Court of Appeal, but it was the additions to the letter which interested King. On the copy paper in a round longhand someone had written:

Gilheaney: No Action
cross refer— Crime Desk
Fair Holiday
Violent Crime
Mr. Justice Morningstar (career of)
McNulty, Spicer and Watson
Court of Appeal (famous cases)

It seemed to King that the *Clarion* had a sophisticated computerized data bank system which might well match anything possessed by the Police force. Either that or the newspaper had a well run conventional cross-indexing system. Bill McGarrigle had followed up a complaint about shady business practices of a city solicitor, had checked his paper's records and had found that that same solicitor had once agreed to represent a man who later claimed that his solicitor had wilfully played a part in his malconviction. The home-loving, book-loving reporter had followed up the lead in order to save his job and in the process had discovered that he was no mean investigative reporter. But he was throwing himself in the deep end, he'd never developed a nose for trouble and it cost him his life.

King left Bill McGarrigle's study and went to the front room. Mrs. McGarrigle was sitting by the empty hearth, looking at nothing with an expression of nothing, nursing a glass of port and mumbling softly to herself. Or maybe, King thought, maybe there was an expression, the wide-eyed awe of a little girl who'd stayed on past her stop and was looking out of the bus window at a strange and fearsome territory.

King turned away and let himself out of the flat.

Montgomerie left Sussock in the canteen and went up to the CID rooms and put a call through to the Isle of Bute police at Rothesay.

"Yet more service for the brave boys from the city," said the desk sergeant when Montgomerie had identified himself.

"What's that supposed to mean, hayseed?" asked Montgomerie.

"Don't get touchy," said the voice. It sounded old and wise. A copper's copper. "In the summertime we don't do anything except collar neds and screwballs who descend upon us from the good city of Glasgow, all with felonious intent."

"You mean you nick them with felonious intent?"

"What can I do for you?" said the voice, suddenly drying up.

"Re, one Spicer, local notable, resident of Bute, some old school house methinks, works as a mouthpiece in sinful city of G."

"I know him," said the desk sergeant, whose voice sounded like something big dragging itself across a drought-stricken riverbed. "What about him?"

"He's under suspicion of being a nasty."

"Oh?" There was not a small hint of undisguised surprise.

"Yes. Can you keep an eye on him and let us know when he leaves the island and what he's driving when he leaves?"

"Sure thing. How much of a nasty is he?"

"A very nasty nasty."

Montgomerie put the 'phone down and lit a fag. Before he was half way to the filter his telephone rang.

"Just confirming your identity," said the dried-up voice from Bute.

"Oh, I'm the genuine article all right."

"I sent a Panda to drive past his house," said the desk sergeant. "Spicer's on the island at the moment. He doesn't look like he's going anywhere tonight, he's got less than an hour to catch the last ferry to the mainland and at the moment he's dressed in boxer shorts hosing down his fleet of high-class motors. He could get the Tighnabruaich ferry later tonight but that would leave him with a one-hundred-mile drive to Glasgow."

"Thanks," said Montgomerie.

"We'll watch every ferry tomorrow."

"Thanks again."

Montgomerie took a bleeper from the stores and went back up to the West End. He sat in a tough gin-bin protecting his bruised ribs by sitting against a wall. He felt awkward, clumsy, consumed with guilt, wondering how long before it all came out about his visit to Tiny Jardine's. The one thing he was sure of was that he had to tell Donoghue before Donoghue found out by other means. He had to take control of the situation, rescue what he could; he couldn't afford to let it all come out in the interview rooms.

It was an old style horseshoe bar with pillars here and there. There were some hard cases, some sad cases, mostly they were men with loud voices and big stomachs. There were one or two women, shiny black skirts, tights like sand sprinkled with gold dust.

"You into business?"

"Beat it, sister."

Richard King was home in time to spend an hour with his children before they had to be in bed. They built a tower with coloured plastic bricks which squeaked when pressed. The most they could manage was seven in a column.

Later he sat talking with his Quaker wife and when she rose to percolate some coffee he watched her walk across the room.

He wondered what sort of man could murder a girl and then marry her sister. How could he find it in himself to lie with her at night? How could he free his conscience so much that he didn't have to worry about talking in his sleep or half-sleep? How, how could he?

10

FAIR Monday.

It was the heat that awoke Donoghue as he lay naked under a single sheet. The heat and the birds and the light which streamed through a chink in the curtains and let Donoghue see that at 6.00 a.m. the sky was already blue and cloudless. He rolled out of bed, adjusted the sheet and pummelled the pillows. He poured a glass of orange juice and awoke properly in a lukewarm bath. He sat at the breakfast bar in the kitchen and ate muesli and fruit and drank a mug of coffee.

The post came on time, as did the newspaper: it wasn't a public holiday in Edinburgh. He folded the *Scotsman* under his arm, left two official-looking envelopes on the hall table and walked back to the kitchen reading the reverse of a postcard from Scarborough. It said:

Dear Daddy,
We are having a very good time.
We are sorry you could not come

with us at the last minute.
Mummy sends her love.

      Timmy and Louisa
PS. Louisa caught three crabs
yesterday.

He drove to Glasgow. He enjoyed the drive, the visibility was good, the air seemed clean and fresh and the Fair holiday meant the traffic was light. He drove in the inside lane all the way listening to Radio Four. He turned off the motorway at Charing Cross and parked his car at the rear of "P" Division police station. At 8.29 he was at his desk, he flicked his gold-plated cigarette lighter and started pulling on his first pipe of the day.

Montgomerie arose gingerly, well aware of the delectable Fiona smiling at his obvious discomfort. He washed, shaved and dressed as hurriedly as his physical condition would allow. In Fiona's small kitchen he put some jam between two slices of bread and chewed into it while making a pot of tea. He drank half a cup of tea and then left the flat, going down the stair on tiptoe because walking too hard on his heels jarred his ribs. Behind the wheel of his car he suddenly felt light-headed and realized that he was still drunk from the bevvy he'd consumed the previous night. Then the memory of going to see Tiny Jardine came crashing into his mind and it was more than the previous night's drink and his damaged ribs which caused him to stagger slightly as he entered "P" Division at 8.32 a.m. He made a mug of black coffee in the canteen and carried it up to the CID rooms on the first floor.

Richard King awoke and found that in the night Iain had climbed on to their bed and had fallen asleep between him and Rosemary. He moved gently out of the bed and opened the windows wider to let out the smell of paint and paste which King knew gave Rosemary a headache and about which she never complained. He made a pot of tea and carried a mug through to the bedroom for his wife, and found that in his absence she had lifted the still sleeping Iain into bed with her. He breakfasted quickly but without bolting his food and drove into the city, arriving at "P" Division within sixty seconds of Montgomerie.

Ray Sussock had had a hard time. He had stayed in the canteen long after

Montgomerie had left, waiting for the time that the sun stopped slamming down and might begin to shine gently, benignly, with hopefully a little breeze to cool sweating brows. But it stayed up there well after 7.00 p.m., top dog. Without a car of his own and with only 53p in cash Sussock was forced to walk from "P" Division to his bedsit in the West End, hopping from shade to shade, trying not to think about the pain in his stomach and the unnerving weakness in his wrists and legs.

In his flat he pulled open the top drawer of his dresser. It was the drawer where he kept his "odd" important possessions: passport, health card, driving licence, insurance policy. He rummaged until he found a bronze ring with three keys threaded on it.

He had gone down to Highburgh Road and jumped a 59 bus to take him across the city. His 53p was just enough to get him to the south side, to Langside, to a room and kitchen with "Willems" bolted to the door. Just a can of beans would do, maybe with a bit of bread, perhaps even an egg on top. He knew she kept a supply of cans since the incident when she was stranded in her flat in Stranraer one winter, laid up ill, no one called on her and she ran out of food.

Sussock had grappled with his set of keys to her flat, moving from top to bottom unlocking the three locks on her door, clumsy with desperation, and succeeded in opening the door two inches because that was as far as the anti-break-in chain would allow. It was a natty piece of ironmongery allowing the house-owner to apply it on leaving the house, and release it by unlocking it with a key which was poked round the side of the door frame to get out the lock.

Sussock didn't have that key. That was the only one he didn't have. That was the only key she didn't have a spare of. That was one of the things she kept meaning to do, old Sussock, I really must get a spare chain key just in case. Ray Sussock had sat on the stair and for the first time in a long time felt like throwing a tantrum. He had felt that it was all against him. Him. For everybody else and their neat well-adjusted lives, and against him. God knows he didn't want any favours, no preferential treatment, but the odd break in life wouldn't have gone amiss. Why, he had wondered, was it only his journey that was uphill? Why had it all come to this, from the tough streets of the old Gorbals, to being a detective-sergeant (and that only because of length of service and nothing else), to living with the screwballs in bedsit land, a wife who was off her head and an only son who was a pansy, and now only a few inches of shiny brass chain between him and a can of beans.

It had occurred to him to break the door down and the more he thought about it, the more it had loomed as a big possibility. Just a gentle nudge with his shoulder and it would be feasting time. It wouldn't take much, he was a big man, he would just need to lean on it, there would hardly be any damage, and she wouldn't mind . . .

But it was breaking and entering and he was an officer of the law. That made it tough for him to get away with questionable activities in the grey area of the law, where actions may or may not be illegal, where discretion can be exercised. At all times he had to be above suspicion if he wanted to collect his pension, and at his age his pension was his meal ticket. He had no time for bent dicks but in his thirty-plus years' service he'd seen too many good coppers lose everything because they had chewed into an apple while attending a break-in at a grocer's. Above suspicion.

He had locked her door and walked homewards. On the way he met a beggar who asked him for money. "Why not, friend?" said Sussock and gave him all he had, seven new pence. For the rest of his journey in a starry and balmy night he had experienced that strange sense of freedom which comes when you haven't anything left to lose.

Sussock had slept on his stomach that night to reduce the hunger pains. He walked to the police station on Fair Monday arriving at 8.38 a.m. He asked to borrow some coffee and made it strong and heavy on the milk. He went upstairs to the CID rooms, raised a hand in greeting to King and Montgomerie and went down the corridor to his own office. He felt badly weakened but if he could avoid strenuous exercise he might be OK.

The review meeting in Donoghue's office commenced at 8.45 a.m. sharp.

"Developments?" asked Donoghue, pulling on his pipe. "Jug and Steamroller Forbes were seen talking to Phil Jardine yesterday, later afternoon, on Byres Road," said Montgomerie, anxious to please, savouring each moment, feeling his days in the force were numbered.

"Significance?"

"Only that they were in the West End confirms what Cleopatra McCusker told us."

"It doesn't confirm anything. It ties in neatly with what she told DC King but it's not a confirmation. Did they see you?"

"Yes, sir. I followed Jug but he gave me the slip."

Sussock grunted.

"Well actually," confessed Montgomerie, "I let him go when I saw he was leading me a merry dance."

"So they are alert to our interest in them?"

"No more than usual, sir," said King. "I've been watching them for months now and they know I've been watching them; in fact we've been circling each other like a couple of scorpions. I don't think that they know we know about the planned bank raid on Tuesday morning, because from what DC Montgomerie has just said it sounds as though they were not too upset about being seen. I think that if they thought we had advance warning of a specific job they'd cancel everything and go into hibernation."

"But they seem to be going for launch." Donoghue leaned backwards.

"Exactly, sir. They must be assuming that Cleopatra McCusker hasn't coughed."

"Good. You'll be back up in the West End today, Montgomerie?"

"Yes, sir. I've contacted the police on the Isle of Bute to let us know if Spicer leaves the island. It occurred to me that if we could follow him in the city he might lead us to the safe house."

"Now that, Montgomerie," said Donoghue, "is the sort of initiative I like to see in my officers. Well done."

Montgomerie shifted in his seat.

"King?"

"Well, sir." King cleared his throat. "I think I just need to feed back for DC Montgomerie's benefit. It seems that Anne McDonald, who by this time was calling herself Forbes-McDonald, was blackmailing Spicer. He employed her as his secretary and she soon tumbled to his less than honest approach to his clients' monies."

"So she angled for a cut?"

"That's right. Got it her way too, apparently. She seemed a wealthy lassie, she kidded on she had a rich old man. These are transcripts of her letters." King passed them to Montgomerie and handed copies to Donoghue and Sussock. "Bill McGarrigle got on to the Gilheaney issue after following through the cross-indexing in the *Clarion*'s filing system. Gilheaney wrote to the *Clarion* from the nick and the filing system showed Spicer to have been his brief. Bill McGarrigle was already working on Spicer, and so followed up Gilheaney's allegation."

Donoghue tapped ash from his pipe bowl in the large black ashtray which stood on his desk.

"My guess is," continued King, "that Bill McGarrigle was too overt in his approach, probably even tried to interview Spicer. Spicer by this time was ingratiating himself with the Jardines and had hired his own hit man, Neutron John McCusker. He probably asked McCusker to have a few words with McGarrigle and warn him off."

Donoghue nodded, he could picture the scene. Bill McGarrigle walking up and down Rutherglen Main Street at nearly midnight

246

and still naïvely waiting for Samantha Simonds to show. He was approached by a stocky character in a cloak: Excuse me, sir, are you the gentleman asking about Mr. Spicer? . . . Well there's someone wants to meet you, this way, sir, in the back court, just through this close here, sir, after you, sir. Maybe, thought Donoghue, maybe it was like that. Or maybe McCusker got a message to McGarrigle: Be in these particular backs at midnight for information about Spicer. Just wait there, you'll be contacted. Whichever trick McCusker had used he'd come out of the incident a murderer.

"Well," said Donoghue, holding his pipe in both hands, "for my part I have spoken to the pathologist who informs me that Anne McDonald's injuries could have been inflicted by a person who has use only of his left arm and hand. Given this information and the information dug up by DC King which provides a motive, we have to assume that Spicer is the prime suspect in the McDonald killing."

"It's looking nice and black for Spicer," said Montgomerie.

"It's looking black for the police force,"

mumbled Sussock, but nobody heard him, or if they did, nobody responded.

"Not black enough," replied Donoghue. "Remember he's a lawyer. If we confront him now he'll wriggle away."

"We've got enough on him to give grounds on a fraud charge," said King.

"We'll not get a murder conviction out of that." Donoghue put his pipe between his teeth. "No, we have to watch him further. I like DC Montgomerie's idea. Montgomerie, you'll spend the rest of the day in the West End, Ray and King you'll take an unmarked car and wait at the Wemyss Bay ferry terminal and pick up Spicer when and if he comes to the mainland. If he comes today he won't be going to his office, so Montgomerie's guess about him going to the safe house is likely to be right. If we haven't made any progress by midnight we'll have to alert the bank and wait for them in Maryhill tomorrow morning."

"If we do that," said King, "we'll only collar the neds. Again."

"Right." Donoghue nodded. "So we need action this day if we're going to pull in Spicer and the Jardines."

Montgomerie walked up to the West End, along Sauchiehall Street, through Kelvingrove Park, and reached Byres Road from University Avenue. He knew the pattern followed by Jardine's thugs, drinking late into the night, rising late in the morning, usually about opening time. Montgomerie reached the West End of the city at 10.30 a.m. He bought a coffee and a bun in a café. He reckoned he had an hour in hand before he need start looking for anyone he recognized.

King enjoyed the drive down the banks of the Clyde and round the tail of the bank to Wemyss Bay. He saw it as one of the perks of the job, and there were damn few of those, piloting an unmarked Granada by the side of the river on a summer's morning, windows and sun roof open, driving in shirtsleeves and shades. King parked outside the railway station at Wemyss Bay and went to the buffet and bought teas and scones for himself and Sussock. Ray Sussock declined to leave the car, so King stood alone at the wall by the ferry terminal, drinking tea, eating his scone, enjoying the sea breeze and watching the shipping in the estuary. It was 10.48 a.m.

Donoghue sat at his desk and read over the file on Spicer. It wasn't yet in any form of order, just a jumble of handwritten reports, duplications, recordings of interviews, newspaper cuttings, an extract from a post mortem report, all sandwiched between two stiff manilla sheets. Donoghue's curiosity was drawn to the source of Spicer's financial problems, his pub, the Fleur de Lys. It was 11.10, it was hot and windless, the city was baking. Usually a man who liked shorts, this day Donoghue fancied a lager, served stingingly cold.

The Fleur de Lys was in the centre of the city, south of the river, near Bridge Street subway station. It was an old building surrounded by demolition sites, shabbily done up to attract the punter who spends, spends, spends; the adolescents trying to be twelve pints a night men, hard men. But the whole place was phoney and cheap, too near waste ground to be trendy, too near the rumbling elevated rails of Glasgow Central to offer escape, and on the wrong side of the river to be fashionable. There were only one or two people in the bar when Donoghue walked in, mostly they were old, some very old. Spicer's clients seemed to be drawn mainly from the isolated elderly who still live in this decaying part of the city and maybe the odd lorry-driver taking a lunch-time pint before going on to the docks to pick up a load. In the bar Donoghue could smell the drains and there was a wide crack running across the length of the ceiling which, with four storeys of stonebuilt tenement above, didn't make Donoghue feel too secure. He ordered a lager and the barman hit him for fifty per cent over inner city prices and even then the drink was flat and warm. It wasn't too difficult to see why Spicer's goldmine was, as McNulty said, haemorrhaging badly.

"Looking for a wee guy called McCusker," said Donoghue, putting the glass back on the gantry and having no intention of picking it up again.

The barman was bending down washing glasses and he looked up at Donoghue with a go to hell expression and said he didn't know of any wee guy called McCusker.

"Sometimes called Neutron John."

The man went on washing glasses in a manner which said very loudly that he knew McCusker alias Neutron John very well.

"The headman in, aye?" persisted Donoghue.

The man looked up again, he had hard eyes in a hard face, a moustache and a beard cut close. He began to look at Donoghue like Glaswegians do when you turn down their offer of a drink: like they're going to eat you whole. "You're looking at him," growled the man.

"That right? Well, I was really wanting Spicer, your boss, *the* head man."

"He's not around. Who's asking?"

"A friend."

"All right, friend, when you find Spicer you tell him his manager wants money."

"He's not paying up, aye?"

"He's not paying nobody, bar staff, suppliers, decorators, brewery, nobody."

"How long has he had the bar?"

"Thought you said you were a friend of him?"

"I'm a recent acquaintance," said Donoghue.

"Two years, good as. The place is falling down. You need to spend money to make money. Spicer, he bought this place for a song and he put a bit of plastic here and there, a space invader machine in one corner and a jukebox in the other, then he reckoned he'd sit back and watch the till fill. You can't do that."

"No?"

"No. If I had a bit of money I'd get a place and I'd spend on it, really spend, I'd be printing money in a few years but I'd work at it. Spicer needs to do that but he won't; this place takes nothing, even on a Friday it takes nothing. I don't know how he's kept it open. I tell you, it's the wrong guys which get the breaks."

"Last thing life is, is fair." Donoghue nodded in agreement.

"You don't need to tell me. I'm quitting soon. Who was it who called?"

"Don't bother," said Donoghue. "I'll be seeing Spicer before the day's out."

He left the Fleur de Lys, walked into the city and grabbed some lunch at a fast food joint.

Montgomerie didn't see any action until 3.00 p.m. He was standing in a lane off Byres Road when Steamroller Forbes lumbered past. Montgomerie's heart missed a beat, he could have reached out and touched him, but Steamroller Forbes went right past. Montgomerie let him go and stepped out after him.

The big man was suffering in the heat. The back of his shirt was saturated, he was dragging one foot in front of the other and barely making headway. His general direction was north, but Montgomerie felt it was touch and go whether Forbes reached Great Western Road before his heart gave out.

But he did make it and hung a right, eastwards towards the city, moving easier in the shade of the buildings. He walked up to the brow of the road and turned into a dark close between a Chinese takeaway and an Indian grocer's. Montgomerie noted the close number and walked on. He crossed the road and walked on the elevated terrace on the north side of Great Western Road, from which he could look into the first-floor windows of the tenements on the south side of the road. He identified the close into which Steamroller Forbes had walked. The first-floor right flat of that close had the curtains drawn shut. The other flats in that close had the curtains open and were airing their stuffy rooms with the windows flung wide.

Montgomerie walked down to the 'phone-box outside the Botanical Gardens and dialled through to Donoghue. "I think I've located the safe house, sir," he said when Donoghue answered. Then he gave details.

"Right, stick with it. I'll be contacting you but probably not for a while." Donoghue replaced the receiver without waiting for Montgomerie's reply and then dialled a three-figure internal number. "Armoury? DI Donoghue. I'll be wanting to draw firearms later today, please . . . four .38s and six rounds apiece. Thank you." He replaced the receiver and sat back in his chair. He was trying to stop his heart from pounding. It was 3.45 p.m.

At Wemyss Bay King and Sussock sat in the Granada. Over the last six hours they had discovered that the action at Wemyss Bay consists solely of a throughput of people, arriving by road or rail for the ferry to Rothesay, or arriving on the ferry and leaving by road or rail. Wemyss Bay comprises a ferry terminus, a rail terminus, a small string of shops, a hotel and a caravan site. After six hours in Wemyss Bay, King's perk had turned into an imposition.

Sussock had spent the entire time sitting in the passenger seat, hardly moving, hardly talking. He knew his behaviour was making King curious and was impressed that the young man had resisted the temptation to pry. He'd been sustained by food which King bought from the railway buffet, the scone this morning, a meat pie at midday, latterly a packet of crisps and, so far, five cups of tea. He felt he was beginning to put upon people, something he wanted to avoid, but now the end was in sight; the rest of the afternoon, the evening, one night and through until 10.00 a.m. in the morning. Eighteen hours, if he could just hang in there.

The radio crackled. "Control to Tango Two Four."

Sussock reached forward and snatched the microphone. He pressed the "send" button and said, "Tango Two Four receiving."

"Tango Two Four. Information received from Isle of Bute police. Suspect John Spicer has embarked on the 4.00 p.m. ferry, arriving your location approx. 4.45 p.m. Suspect is driving white Mercedes estate . . ." the crackling female voice went on to give the car's registration number and to inform that Spicer was the sole occupant. Sussock wrote down the details on his pad and pressed the car's horn. King turned away from reading the names on the war memorial and walked over to the car.

"He's on the next boat," said Sussock.

They picked up Spicer without difficulty and trailed three cars behind as he drove towards Glasgow. Spicer drove slowly and carefully, an easy suspect to follow in a distinctive car and not giving the slightest impression that he knew he was being watched. He crossed the Clyde on the Erskine Bridge, drove down Dumbarton Road into Great Western Road. He turned into Byres Road and parked his car in a side-street. King slowed down and Sussock left the car. King reached forward for the radio transmitter microphone and pressed the "send" button.

"Tango Two Four to control."

"Control speaking." The interference was unusually heavy but the female voice was still easily heard.

"Tango Two Four, suspect now on foot in Byres Road area. Being followed on foot by Detective-Sergeant Sussock."

"Control. Understood Tango Two Four. Please rendezvous with DC Montgomerie on Buckingham Terrace."

King turned a neat U and drove back up Byres Road and on to Buckingham Terrace. He saw Montgomerie standing between two Bentleys and in the shade of a tree. King drove on until he found a hole for the Granada at the kerbside and then walked back to join Montgomerie.

"What news, my son?" he said.

"See the flat with the curtains shut, behind me, first floor?" Montgomerie took his cigarettes from his jacket pocket and offered one to King and took one himself. "That, old pal, is a safe house."

"You've been up the close?"

"You must be joking. I want to live to collect my pension." Then he fell silent.

"Something wrong, Mal?" asked King. "You've gone pale."

"No, nothing," said Montgomerie, forcing a smile. "No, I followed Steamroller Forbes to the close mouth. It's got to be their safe house, the one that Cleopatra McCusker told us about, it's the only flat on the close, on the whole of the terrace in fact, with the curtains shut and on a day like this. It must be like an oven in there."

"You seen anybody at the window?"

"No. They're being careful."

"You're sure they're in there?"

"Aye, I'm sure. Well, pretty sure anyway." Montgomerie inhaled, he looked at the houses and hotels on Buckingham Terrace, at the tall angular buildings in the middle distance to the east, at the blue hills on the western sky line. He looked anywhere but directly across Great Western Road at the flat with the drawn curtains.

"Anyway, we'll find out soon enough," said King. "Me and Ray Sussock followed Spicer into the city, he dumped his swish heap on Byres Road and started hoofing it. Ray's following. Have you noticed how Ray's been quiet these last couple of days?"

"He's upset at sending the wrong guy down the line."

"Maybe. He sat in the car all day, didn't move an eyebrow or say a word. He's not off his grub though, bought him a meat pie and he wolfed it. Licked the crumbs off his hands. Same with the crisps. You know what he did to the bag . . ." King stopped talking and then said, "That's him."

Montgomerie turned. He located Spicer without difficulty, white shirt, slacks carrying a canvas bag, thinly built, a long face locked in a grin, and with a small right arm hanging down. Twenty feet behind him was Ray Sussock.

Spicer turned into the same close that Steamroller Forbes had entered. Ray Sussock walked on past, noting the number as he did so.

"I'll go down and intercept Ray," said King.

"OK. Take a look around the back of the close," replied Montgomerie, dogging his cigarette. "Where's the car?"

King pointed to it and walked briskly to the end of the terrace and down on to Great Western Road. Montgomerie slid into the driving seat and reached for the radio. He called up "P" Division and reported the arrival of Spicer at the safe house. He was ordered to remain on station and await the arrival of the detective-inspector.

"Aye," he said with resignation as he replaced the microphone.

Donoghue's Rover drew up beside him while he was on his second cigarette. Donoghue left his car in the middle of

260

the terrace road and joined Montgomerie. Donoghue stared silently at Montgomerie.

"First-floor right flat directly opposite, curtains shut, sir," said Montgomerie finally, not very quick on the uptake that his senior officer was awaiting a report. "Spicer and Jardine's thug Steamroller Forbes have been seen to go into the close. That flat seems to be the most likely place for them to be." He paused. "No sign of anybody at the window, sir. No other person has been seen to enter or leave the close." He paused again and then said, "DS Sussock and DC King are reconnoitering the rear of the premises, sir."

Donoghue said, "Thank you, Montgomerie. Will you please take my car and put it somewhere legal and then rejoin me?"

"I think you're right," said Donoghue when Montgomerie rejoined him. "The other flats on that stair seem all right. I think the first-floor flat with the curtains shut is looking more and more sinister with each second that passes."

"A right nest of thieves," said Montgomerie.

"It's the two murderers in there,

McCusker and Spicer, that I'm most interested in," replied Donoghue. "Anyway let's get back to my car, they'll smell a rat if they see us hovering here."

They sat in Donoghue's Rover and were joined by Sussock and King. Donoghue noticed Sussock to be walking slowly with his head hanging: like a Jesuit receiving a solemn Mass.

"There's a flat stretch of concrete at the back," said King. "I can't quite make out what it is but it seems to be the roof of an old wash house and trash can alley. Access is easy, down a lane from a side-street, over some backs, over a railing, on to the concrete roof, and the next thing is the kitchen window, big, wide and unbarred. Just waiting for a boot."

"See anybody?"

"No, sir."

"Hear anything?"

"Not a dicky-bird."

"Looks inhabited?"

"Aye. All the curtains of the back rooms are open, so are some of the windows. There's a bottle of milk half full standing on the kitchen table. It looked fresh enough but I didn't get too close."

"Fair enough," said Donoghue. "The next question is, when do we invite ourselves to the party?"

"Right now?" said Montgomerie.

Donoghue turned sideways and looked at him, dragging his eyebrows a millimetre higher as he did so.

"Well," stumbled Montgomerie, "I mean they're in there, all of them. They could disperse . . ." Eventually he fell silent.

"I certainly want them all," conceded Donoghue, "Spicer especially." He looked forward again. "Any advances on immediate action?"

"Any later and they're likely to be full of drink," said King, glancing at his watch. "I mean it's coming up five o'clock already. Pretty soon they'll be full of flight or fight, probably fight."

"So you too would go in immediately?"

"I think so, sir."

"With the knowledge that there's likely to be firearms in there and with all these people on the street?"

"Well . . ."

"You surprise me, King. Ray, your opinion?"

It was Sussock's strongly held personal

opinion that they should go in there and get it over with as soon as possible while he still had strength to muster. But after clearing his throat, he said, "Very early morning would be the best time, I think, sir."

"Suppose Spicer goes in the meantime?"

"I don't think he will."

"Why?"

"He was carrying a bag, an overnight bag I would think."

"That is a significant fact and it wasn't reported," growled Donoghue in voice like iced gravel. He didn't direct the statement but Montgomerie felt particularly uncomfortable.

"Anyway," said Sussock quickly, feeling tension begin to rise in the confines of the car, "he's cutting it pretty fine if he wants to get back to the Isle of Bute tonight. If he doesn't leave within the next ninety minutes he's staying on the mainland tonight."

"Could he sleep anywhere else in the city?"

There was a moment's silence and then King said, "The only other place he could sleep is his weekend retreat in Argyllshire, Clematis Cottage."

264

"He'll not be trekking up there the night," said Sussock.

"So we can assume he's staying in the safe house tonight with his criminal accomplices?" Donoghue turned and looked at the other three, who nodded their agreement. "Good, good," he said as he faced forward. "I'm pleased you agree with me. The raid has been timed for three a.m. We'll be supported by an inspector and a sergeant from the uniformed branch plus twelve constables. Weapons will be drawn. Spicer and his friends should be sound asleep by then, and besides the constables won't be free until well after midnight. A lot of folk will be starting back at work tomorrow morning so there'll be a lot of commiseratory drinking on the town tonight."

"It's a dog's life, a copper's life," said Montgomerie.

"You said something?"

"Nothing, sir."

"Good. So, Montgomerie, you stay here with the unmarked car. Whistle if there's any developments. We'll get back to the station, rest up, grab some food."

Food, thought Sussock, food, food, food.

Montgomerie sat in the unmarked car and adjusted the rear-view mirror so that he looked diagonally across Great Western Road at the safe house. It was a comfortable observation station compared to some he'd been on. Once he'd suffered exposure after observing a farmhouse for twelve hours one winter's day with nothing but a tree for shelter. But despite the comfort of this observation station it did have the problem of all other observation stations: one of unremitting tedium. Tedium allowed Montgomerie's mind to dwell on things, like visiting Tiny Jardine, like an interview with Chief Superintendent Findlater, like his P45 in the morning post, like signing on the dotted line at the Job Centre.

The unremitting boredom was broken only once. At approximately 7.15 a Ford estate car drew up outside the close in which the safe house stood. Montgomerie left the Granada and strolled along Buckingham Terrace until he was directly opposite the safe house but was also partially obscured by a tree. He noted the number of the estate car. Ten minutes later the two men who had arrived in the estate car reappeared on the street; this time they were accompanied by a third man who looked as white as a sheet. The three men got into the estate car and drove off. The third man was Neutron John McCusker.

Montgomerie walked back to the Granada and radioed in to "P" Division.

"I don't think we'll change the plan," Donoghue's voice crackled over the radio. "McCusker won't be going very far. We can pick him up when he surfaces."

Montgomerie remained on station until he was relieved at midnight by King.

The raid was mounted at 0305 hours Tuesday. It was a warm and still night, as dark as a deep twilight with just the faintest crack of dawn visible in the north-east.

Ray Sussock, who had declined to carry a revolver, led a uniformed inspector, who carried a gun, and six constables along a back lane, across a back court and stopped at the railings in front of the concrete roof.

"Just two at a time across the roof," said the inspector. "It doesn't look safe."

Sussock nodded. He began to feel faint. He hadn't given a reason for refusing a firearm but had declined because the lack of food was sapping his strength at a rate of knots. He no longer felt able to hold and point a gun, or if necessary squeeze the trigger. He felt a danger to himself and his colleagues. A senior constable had taken the gun in his place.

The inspector and an unarmed constable inched across the concrete roof and crouched, one at either side of the window. The constable drew his truncheon.

"Wait until we hear the door getting fetched down," murmured the inspector. Then he added, "Steady, lad."

King and Montgomerie edged into the close. They each carried a revolver. Behind them was a sergeant of uniformed branch and six constables. At the rear of the column, taking care not to brush his suit against the wall of the grimy close was Detective-Inspector Donoghue.

King and Montgomerie reached the door of the flat. It was dark, the old, badly maintained close could boast no stair lighting and King took out his pocket torch to shine on the door. The door was solid and old and heavy, no name above the letter-box, three locks, one barrel and two mortice.

"What do you think?" asked King.

A line of policemen stood silently, tensely on the stair. "I think we should give this up and go and knock over the Bank of Scotland," replied Montgomerie without lowering his voice. "Why don't we just knock?"

"Get a grip, Mal!" King was anxious.

"Grip of what? That's just it, nothing to grip—no handle, just keyholes."

"What the hell . . . You didn't bring any keys?"

"Didn't think we'd need any."

"You didn't think we'd . . ." King groaned like an old wooden ship groans for the last time, long and low. "What did you think we're on here, Ding Dong Avon calling?"

"So you're so bloody wise why didn't you bring them?"

"Because I was on observation, remember? And because I'm not a dab hand at getting in and out of people's flats. You've acquired a reputation for that."

"I have?" Montgomerie smiled. "Recognition is so nice." King put his hand to his head. "I can't see the point in going on," he moaned. "This is a job we've got here, Malcolm."

"Mr. Donoghue wants to know what the delay is for, sir," whispered a constable from just behind Montgomerie's head.

"Slight technical hitch," said Montgomerie and he heard "technical hitch" being whispered from mouth to mouth down the stair, culminating in the flicking of a cigarette lighter at the bottom.

"Everybody's so calm," moaned King.

"We need skill for this," said Montgomerie.

"Oh, you are working for us, then?" King said.

"Skill, expertise, knowledge, experience," chanted Montgomerie.

"Mal, it's three-ten. Ray Sussock will be wondering if he's got the right gaff."

"Skill," said Montgomerie. "Do we have McMullen in our team?"

"Aye, we do," sighed King.

"McMullen!" hissed Montgomerie. "Up here!"

A big shape loomed out of the shadows, moved up lightly and crouched silently beside Montgomerie, no mean feat since McMullen stood six seven, weighed eighteen stone and was full back in the Strathclyde Police first fifteen.

"What do you think?" asked Montgomerie.

"Skill," sighed King, playing the beam of his torch over the locks for McMullen's edification.

"Tough one, this one," said McMullen slowly, tapping a lock two-thirds of the way down the door. "I know locks like this, they're basically a bar of steel a foot long, half an inch thick and three inches deep. They extend four or five inches into the door frame. You lock and unlock them with three or four turns of the key."

"Don't get locks like that these days," said Montgomerie. "They had big problems with housebreaking in the days when these houses were built."

"That right?"

"Aye, nothing's new," said McMullen.

King sank back against the wall and made a sound like there was a cat trapped in his stomach.

"Any of you gents got a penknife," asked the mountainous McMullen. Montgomerie handed him a knife. "Small blade," he said apologetically.

"It's big enough." McMullen stood and began prodding the door at the other side.

"Aye, like I thought," he said. "It's turned to driftwood. One good blow should fetch the hinges off, but watch the door falling. They weigh a ton."

"OK," said Montgomerie. "Ready when you are."

McMullen went to the far side of the landing and ran at the door, leading with his shoulder. There was a rendering, splintering sound, McMullen bounced backwards, plaster fell from the walls and from the next landing up, and inside the flat somebody shouted and a window smashed. The door stayed where it had always been.

"That's Ray going in," King said.

"Again!" yelled Montgomerie.

McMullen ran at the door a second time and this time it gave. He pushed it open, splintering the wood round the hinges and bending the old metal in the locks, forcing a gap of three feet between the door and the frame. Montgomerie and King went in, groping in the dark. There was a flashlight at the far end of the hallway, maybe thirty feet away. "Police!" yelled a voice from behind the light.

"It's us!" replied King. The flashlight was turned away. King went into a room on his right, Montgomerie followed him, switching on the light. They pointed their guns at an empty room.

"Where the hell are they?" yelled Montgomerie.

"I don't know," screamed King.

They went back into the hall. Somebody yelled, "In here!" They moved forward as a man came running out of a room on the left of the corridor, fists flailing, and naked except for underpants. He collided with Montgomerie, who hissed as pain jabbed his bruised ribs. He threw the man to the floor and sat on him while he snapped on the handcuffs.

Somewhere a woman screamed. Two thugs ran into the corridor. King held up his gun. "Against the wall! Move!" Somebody found the light switch just as Steamroller Forbes and Jug McLintock backed against the wall. The light came on just in time for King to see the colour drain from their faces.

"I'm arresting you," said Montgomerie, hauling the man to his feet, "for assaulting a police officer in the course of his duties. That'll do for now. Constable!" The man was hustled down the stair and into the waiting van, as were Jug McLintock and Steamroller Forbes.

King went into the room from which Jug McLintock and Steamroller Forbes had emerged. There were three beds in the room and Sam "the Weight" Dolan was staggering out of the third, sleepy and drunk. "Keep on coming," said King.

In the main bedroom of the house Spicer was sharing a bed with a blonde girl. They lay blinking at the policemen, Spicer resting on his good arm and holding the undersized version across his eyes as a shade from the light-bulb. The girl pulled the sheet up to her throat and looked like she wanted her mummy. There was a big loud silence until Donoghue edged his way into the room and said, "How old is she, Spicer?"

"Sixteen. She's sixteen!" His voice was like a storm in the night, howling in every direction.

"She'd better be, Spicer," said Donoghue. "Mind you, in your case it's academic. You're washed up and finished."

"I want to make a statement," Spicer said. Even though he was frightened, on edge, his face was still fixed in a grin, like a death's head mask.

274

"I'm sure we can accommodate that request," snarled Sussock.

"What are you arresting me for, Officer? You have to arrest me." He was beginning to recover. "I won't go anywhere unless you arrest me."

"Conspiracy to murder," said Donoghue.

"Who, who?"

"William McGarrigle, the reporter."

"Oh yes, I read about that. Struck me as being an offence of culpable homicide at the most. Anyway, how do you tie me in?"

"Via Neutron John McCusker."

"Never heard of him."

"That isn't what Mrs. McCusker says."

"These are all strange names to me, Mr—er—"

"Donoghue. Would you like to make a statement about the armed robbery which you had planned for later this morning, with a little help from the Jardine brothers and the thugs outside? That would be conspiracy to rob with violence."

"Really, Mr. Donoghue, this is all too fanciful."

"You think so? Do you want legal advice? How about calling your senior partner,

McNulty? I'm sure he'd like to chat abou
your company's accounts."

"You won't touch me so easily, Officer.

"Excuse me, sir."

Donoghue turned.

"Firearms in the kitchen, sir."

"Right," said Donoghue, "put a man o
them. Nobody to touch them until Forensi
get here." He turned back to Spicer. "
hope you were able to resist the temptatio
to touch those guns."

"I was examining material evidence for
client."

"Don't give us that cat meat," growle
Sussock.

"The onus of proof rests with you," sai
Spicer, now grinning with his eyes as well.

"I know my job," said Donoghue
"We've been doing some digging, we've go
spadefuls of gold dust on you."

"Such as?"

"The murder of Anne McDonald. A few
months before you married her sister."

"How the hell did you find out abou
that?"

"Neatest confession I ever heard," sai
Sussock.

Donoghue drove down to "P" Division. He reached it at 4.00 a.m. when the sky was grey with blue round the edge. He approached the desk sergeant and asked that he pass a message to Forensic to attend the house on Great Western Road.

"Can't immediately, sir."

"Oh."

"No, sir. Jimmy Bothwell's over at Bishopbriggs. So is Dr. Reynolds."

"Murder?"

"Dead body at any rate. They asked that I ask you to attend as soon as possible, sir."

"I can't. I've got the Spicer case to wrap up, that'll likely take the rest of the day."

"You're the senior officer on duty, sir."

"Who's at Bishopbriggs from the CID?"

"Abernethy, sir. Very inexperienced."

"I know. All right, where in Bishopbriggs are they?"

Donoghue arrived at the scene of the crime at 4.30 a.m. Already in attendance were two Panda cars, a mobile incident room, three unmarked cars, one of which Donoghue recognized as Dr. Reynold's Volvo. A milk-float rattled past, its driver peering at the scene. Donoghue left his car and strode to where a black sheet was laid out on some waste ground. He was pulling and blowing on his pipe and was met by Dr. Reynolds.

"Male, apparent age thirty-six years. Time of death, possibly six or eight hours."

"Quite fresh then?"

"Yes, hardly cold."

"Cause of death?" Donoghue took his pipe from his mouth and made to put it in his pocket, but the bowl was too hot so he laid it on the top of a low stone wall which stood beside him.

"Gunshot wounds to the head, I would think," said Reynolds. "I can't be certain until I've done a complete PM."

"Seems pretty certain to me," said Donoghue, smiling. "I mean, if a bloke has a big hole in the side of his head, then . . ."

"It's at the front actually," replied Reynolds. "And it came out at the back. But we might find, for instance, that his heart was already very still before he was shot, in which case we'd have to look elsewhere for the cause of death."

"All right," conceded Donoghue wearily.

"I'd like to take him away and start poking around inside if I may."

"I'll check with Abernethy," said

Donoghue. "I dare say it'll be all right. Oh, incidentally that PM you were about to do when I saw you on Sunday, was it a knife attack?"

"No. He drowned. I can't account for the marks on his body but they didn't contribute to the death."

"Thanks. I was curious." Donoghue walked over to where Abernethy was standing. Abernethy was looking shaky and green round the gills.

"First murder?"

"In CID. Yes, sir."

"Found by?"

"Gentleman in the next house down, sir. Came home very early this morning from his Fair weekend holiday. Saw some stray dogs sniffing at something and investigated."

"Any I/D?"

"I didn't touch the body too much, sir."

"I see. Well, I suggest you leave a man here to keep the public off this stretch of ground until we know we're not looking for a murder weapon, or until we find out what sort of weapon we are looking for. Then I suggest you accompany Dr. Reynolds to the pathology lab and go through the dead man's clothing in an attempt to determine his identity."

"Yes, sir."

"Stay until Dr. Reynolds has completed the PM so that you can bring me his preliminary findings. He may allow you to witness the PM."

"Yes, sir."

"Then a full report on my desk A.S.A.P, complete with photographs and PM report."

"Yes, sir."

Donoghue walked across to where the body lay. It was mostly covered with a sheet and the sick sweet smell of the Grim Reaper was just beginning to rise. Jimmy Bothwell, the forensic assistant, diligent but always awkward in his movements, was calmly taking the dead man's fingerprints. He'd seen it all before. This was just one more stiff.

"Work for you in a house on Great Western Road as soon as you've finished here, Bothwell," said Donoghue. "Details from the desk sergeant."

11

"ABOUT fifteen to twenty years I would say," said Donoghue in response to Spicer's question. "Nearer twenty, I would think, but you know as much about sentencing patterns in these matters as I do."

"Twenty years." Spicer's face was still fixed in a grin but his eyes were no longer smiling. "But it's still the period after that which bothers me. I mean, I'll never re-establish myself."

"That's your problem, Spicer," said Donoghue.

"I suppose things will work out." Spicer sat back in the chair and looked up at the dull white ceiling of the interview room. "See, ten years from now I'll still be in my fifties. With the right breaks I could get out in time to make a bit of money before I'm too old to work. I won't have any capital to come back to, that'll all be taken up in paying clients and creditors, but I'll start somehow. I won't end my life depending on the state pension."

"You don't have any guilt feelings at all, do you, Spicer?"

"I try not to, Mr. Donoghue. Guilt is a useless and a negative emotion. It's a dangerous emotion as well: a lot of stupid and impulsive actions spring from guilty feelings."

"I don't suppose you have any conscience either?"

"I try not to let things dwell on my brain."

"I bet you don't."

"Am I mad or bad? Is that what you are thinking, Mr. Donoghue?"

"The thought had crossed my mind."

"Rest assured, I'm quite sane and I wouldn't want to give you any other impression. Do you want to know what I'm thinking at the moment? I'm thinking that I ought not to have started embezzling the monies from the firm because once I started I couldn't stop. It was especially difficult as I had to cover up every twelve months for the audit, and so it was inevitable that I would be discovered sooner or later. I also wish that I had hired someone a little more professional to kill the reporter. I am further thinking that I ought to have retained my composure when you entered my room earlier today and not have admitted killing Anne McDonald. Until then everything you had against me was circumstantial."

"In fact you don't regret doing any of it, you only regret not getting away with it."

"Exactly."

"You're a bastard, Spicer."

"You're not the first person to say that to me and I dare say you won't be the last. Incidentally, you will by now have found that the girl was over the age of consent."

"By two weeks. You were cutting that fine."

"Perhaps. Perhaps I've been sleeping with her for some time. Either way you'll never find out."

"To think people have been coming to a rat like you with their problems."

"And I just sat there and took all their money. I know, I know, but the weak will always go to the wall."

"So now it's your turn. I think there's a nice ring of justice about that."

"I don't think I've gone to the wall. Everybody's life has its ups and downs and I'm just about to start a low period, but I'll get back up again. Think positively, Mr. Donoghue."

"That's a difficult thing to do in your company, Spicer."

"Maybe. This conversation is getting circular. Do you want me to sign that thing or don't you?"

"I think you'd better," snarled Donoghue. "I'll read it over for you."

"You needn't bother. I murdered Anne McDonald because she was threatening to expose my embezzlement of the firm's money. I also, rather skilfully I think, transferred suspicion on to an innocent person. I hired the man McCusker and instructed him to murder the reporter, McGarrigle." Spicer took his statement and signed it with a ballpoint pen provided by Donoghue. "I suppose that was what gave you your break."

"What was?" Donoghue took the statement and slid it into a manilla folder. He put the ballpoint in his jacket pocket.

"The way I reacted to the reporter. I suppose I was getting scared by then, but I should have brassed it out. He'd have sniffed around and probably come up with one or two points of peripheral interest, but nothing he could go to the law with. Then he would have got bored and gone away. Still, I suppose it's easy to be wise after the event."

"That's always the way, Spicer," said Donoghue. "We'll be sending a report to the Procurator Fiscal. You'll be appearing before the Glasgow Sheriff this morning and we'll be moving for you to be held in custody pending your appearance at the High Court charged with murder. We will be opposing bail."

"I won't be applying for it," said Spicer, with his face fixed in a ridiculous grin and his little right arm hanging by his side. "And now, Mr. Donoghue, I have two requests to make."

"You have two what to make!"

"Requests," said Spicer calmly.

"You're not in much of a position to make requests."

"On the contrary. I have co-operated fully with you. I have confessed to all my sins and I intend to throw myself on the mercy of the court. I feel I can make requests."

"Go on," said Donoghue drily. "But no promises."

"Firstly, I should like my wife to be

brought here to my cell in this police station so that I can tell her that it was I who killed her sister."

"You think she'd like that?"

"No. It will be painful for her. She may even like to assault me, and if she does I would request that you do not intervene until she has scratched my face a little; it would help her. But that would certainly be better than her finding out about it in a newspaper."

"So there is a faint glimmer of humanity about you, after all."

"My wife will be all right. The house on the Isle of Bute is in her name and there is a considerable sum of money in a building society account which is also in her name. I shall lose everything that is in my name but my wife will remain comfortably off. She ought to be happy; she got out of the Saracen, which was all she really wanted."

"You said you had two requests."

"Yes. Secondly, I request the opportunity to turn Queen's Evidence."

Donoghue sat forward.

"I should like to make a statement which would incriminate the Jardine brothers."

"You've already done that." Donoghue

tapped the manilla folder. "In here you say that you and the Jardines planned the bank robbery which was to have taken place this morning."

"There's more. You have access to the accounts we have in the firm. I would draw your attention to the accounts of a company called Deneave Holdings Ltd."

Donoghue scribbled on his notepad.

"If you were to check the records held at Company House you will find that the owners of Deneave Holdings Ltd are Phil and Tiny Jardine. You will also find that Deneave Holdings Ltd is a conglomerate of organizations, one of which is the Delayney's Bar chain here in the city. If further you were to check back the accounts for the six years that they have been held with the firm you will see that periodically there have been massive deposits which coincide in both amount and date with the raids which have been attributed to the Jardines."

"You've been laundering their money?"

"Yes. It's all there in neat columns of figures."

"How did you camouflage it?"

"It was put into three or four different

banks. Sometimes I held on to it for a while and credited the accounts of individual clients just prior to the annual audit. The Jardines saved my bacon a few times like that, by pulling a job a couple of months before the audit. We developed a sort of symbiotic relationship. I needed them and they needed me."

"Seems to me like you gave yourself so much rope you'd hang yourself, eventually."

"Yes, it was a fairly complex system, but anything which baffled the auditors helped me. Anyway it's all there in black and white, as I said. It's enough in itself to nail the Jardines but I am prepared to speak to it from the witness-box if need be."

"Why are you doing this?" asked Donoghue. "Once you do this you'll need protection from the Jardines, even in prison. You'll have to go on Rule 43."

"Perhaps I'm doing it to assist my career as a prisoner," said Spicer, smiling with his eyes again. But there was also a glazed look in the man's eyes which worried Donoghue. "You see, my sentences will run concurrently so the one I have to worry about is the charge of murder. It was a premeditated attack, which could mean a twenty-year term, as you have already said, and so I have to set about reducing it. Initially, I will instruct my counsel to enter a plea in mitigation to the effect that I was being blackmailed and that I tried to atone by marrying the girl's sister and spending lavishly on her."

"That's untrue!" snapped Donoghue. "You married Carol McDonald to remove any last suspicion of you being the man who murdered her sister."

"That may be your opinion, Mr. Donoghue. It may also be the opinion of others, but since nobody can disprove my claim I may be given the benefit of the doubt, especially as I have confessed willingly to everything and have, in addition, turned Queen's Evidence, which should lead to the arrest of a highly successful gang of organized criminals. Altogether that should get me a big reduction in sentence, say five years, so already we are down to a fifteen-year stretch."

"I wouldn't bank on it, Spicer. Especially as you set up an innocent man and watched him go down."

"The responsibility for that miscarriage of justice rests on the shoulders of the Fiscal's office and the Courts, not with me. However, to continue; the admission of my guilt and the turning of Queen's Evidence will lie on my file and will eventually become available to the parole board. I will apply for parole after five years. I won't get it the first time, nobody does, but the sooner I start applying the sooner I'll get it. At any rate I should get remission for good behaviour because I intend to be a model prisoner. All in all, I expect to serve about ten years, the majority of which will be spent in an open prison. That is survivable."

8.30 a.m. Donoghue left the interview room and walked to the front desk. He was tired, slow in his movements and his eyelids were heavy. He had been on duty for exactly twenty-four hours but his tiredness didn't stop him from being pleased to see that WPC Elka Willems was back on duty. As he acknowledged the tall blonde girl he was reminded of the shock waves which went through "P" Division when she stepped over the threshold for the first time. Also entering the building as Donoghue approached the front desk was Chief

Superintendent Findlater, his huge frame almost filling the narrow doorway.

"Good morning, good morning, Fabian." Findlater approached Donoghue. "It's a glorious day. Did you get any holiday at all, Fabian? You know, I hated leaving you with that newspaperman's murder, but I was confident you could handle it."

"I got out a bit, sir," said Donoghue, falling into step with Findlater who led him away from the front desk. "I went to Rothesay, on the Isle of Bute."

"Good, good. I was golfing. St Andrews, very enjoyable. A man needs a break from time to time, Fabian."

"Indeed he does, sir," said Donoghue with forced enthusiasm. "There's one or two things for your attention, sir. I'd particularly like to draw your attention to a memo I wrote to you requesting your approval to re-open the case of Jack Gilheaney."

"Gilheaney . . . I don't recall."

"I'll come along and chat about it, sir."

"And I'm hardly in the door. No rest for the wicked, eh, Fabian?"

Donoghue held open a door for Findlater.

"We have a murder at Bishopbriggs. Abernethy's on it at the moment."

"Have you identified the body?"

"Not yet, sir. I was just going to enquire of the desk sergeant whether Abernethy had contacted us yet."

"I see. What about the newspaper man—what was his name? McGinty?"

"McGarrigle, sir."

"Yes, him. Any developments?"

"We have identified the suspect but we haven't arrested him yet, a man by the name of McCusker. We have also arrested a man who has confessed to be an accomplice to the McGarrigle murder. He has also confessed to a series of other crimes including the Fair Friday murder."

"The Fair Friday murder. We sent someone down for that."

"Yes, sir. Gilheaney, sir."

"Oh dear," said Findlater. "I think you'd better come to my office for a chat, Fabian."

"I'd be pleased to," said Donoghue drily.

"So Spicer's safely under lock and key," said Findlater after Donoghue had finished relating the events of the Fair weekend.

292

'McCusker's still on the run and we might have enough to move against the Jardines."

"Well, we have only Spicer's word that they were party to the planned bank raid. They will deny it completely and they were careful not to let their fingerprints get on any of the weapons we found in the safe house. We haven't yet followed up Spicer's claim about the accounts of Deneave Holdings Ltd, but if it does check out, then that's bad news for the Jardines."

"You'll be getting on to that today?"

"I'll be setting the inquiry in motion, sir. I won't be attending to it personally."

"So long as it's done."

The telephone on Findlater's desk rang. Findlater grasped it in his huge hand and put the receiver to his ear. "Yes," he said, "he's here."

Donoghue took the 'phone and listened. Eventually he said, "Right, get back here and come to the Chief Superintendent's office. You'll have to report verbally. Ask Dr. Reynolds to send his report on as soon as he can, please." Donoghue replaced the receiver. "That was Abernethy," he said. "There was no I/D on the deceased's clothes and so he had to wait until the fingerprints had been processed."

"Which revealed him to be?"

"Neutron John McCusker," said Donoghue. "He was shot through the head but had also sustained some interesting marks on his person."

"Such as?"

"I don't know. Abernethy wouldn't elaborate and he sounded pretty excited, so I didn't press him."

"I hope he calms down before the meeting."

"I'm sure he will. Do you mind if I use your 'phone, sir? If I'm lucky I'll catch King and Montgomerie before they sign out."

The meeting was convened at 9.05 a.m. shortly after Abernethy had returned from the Royal Infirmary. Chief Superintendent Findlater was "the chair", Elka Willems took the minutes, Abernethy was fresh-faced and nervous, Donoghue, King and Montgomerie were bleary-eyed.

"Take your time, lad," said Findlater in his slow Highland accent.

"Well, yes, sir," stammered Abernethy. He was in his early twenties, and even had a residual trace of acne. He consulted his notebook. "The deceased was discovered on a piece of waste ground early this morning. He has since been identified as one Bernie McCusker, alias Neutron John, who I believe is wanted in connection with the murder of Bill McGarrigle."

"That's correct," grunted Findlater.

"There was no identification on the body, that is, I mean, on his clothing, no wallet or anything, and so we had to wait until we could process his fingerprints on the computer, that's what the delay . . ."

"That's all right," said Donoghue supportingly.

"He was killed by a firearm wound to the head. The pathologist, Dr. Reynolds, remarked that it was almost a classic straight between the eyes shot."

"Almost?" Findlater looked at Abernethy.

"Well, the bullet entered the man's head about here." Abernethy tapped the centre of his own forehead. It seemed to Donoghue to be quite a comic gesture, but maybe that was fatigue getting the better of him. He knew from experience that the serious can seem amusing when one is tired. He coughed to stop himself from smiling.

Abernethy continued, "I suppose the doctor meant that the point of entry was a bit high to be called between the eyes . . ."

"Anything else of relevance," asked Findlater, with a sourness which surprised Donoghue.

Abernethy turned the page in his notebook. "Well, I suppose the most significant thing would be the marks on the body of the deceased. They are burns."

"Burns?" It was Montgomerie. He was very frightened that he knew what Abernethy was going to say.

"Yes, sir."

"Don't call DC Montgomerie 'sir', lad," said Findlater. "Carry on."

"Yes, sir. There were about twenty of them, sustained just before he was killed. The pathologist could tell that because some of the burns, what would have been the last two or three to be inflicted, did not go very deep into the skin tissue."

"Death prevented further damage, you mean?"

"Apparently, yes, sir. On some of the burns the damage did extend quite deeply. Damage there was as full as would have been expected, apparently."

"Significance?" asked Donoghue.

"Well . . ." Abernethy began to fidget. "Well, apparently the burns were inflicted over a long period, four or five hours thought the doctor. He thinks the deceased must have been in great pain when he died. Time of death was about eleven p.m. yesterday."

"What time did you see McCusker leave the safe house, Montgomerie?" Donoghue turned to him.

"Approximately seven-fifteen p.m. yesterday."

"The burns had a distinctive mark, sir," Abernethy continued. "A sort of R with a bar through it."

"That should help us." Findlater sat back in his chair.

"There's a few other points which Dr. Reynolds asked me to relate to the meeting." Abernethy looked down at his notebook. "Carpet fibres found underneath the deceased's toenails match some of the fibres found on his clothing. There are rope burns to the deceased's wrists, traces of cotton in his mouth, especially between the teeth . . . oh yes, the gun was fired at point blank range, there's burn marks round the entry wound. There's a big exit wound and the doctor says that if we find the deceased's brains he would be interested in having a look. There was no damage to the deceased's clothing. That's about it, sir. Dr. Reynolds will be forwarding his report as soon as it's typed."

"Thank you. Significance of this information?" asked Findlater.

"McCusker was taken from the safe house yesterday evening by two of Tiny Jardine's thugs," said Montgomerie. "He was taken to Tiny Jardine's ranch-style bungalow near Barrhead. His clothes were taken from him, he was bound and gagged and tortured with branding irons which Tiny Jardine had brought back from a trip he had made to the States. Apparently they once belonged to a ranch called the Split R. We'll probably find that the fibres under McCusker's toenails came from Tiny Jardine's carpet. McCusker was being tortured in order to make him say what he had advertised about his involvement with the Jardine organization. Eventually he was shot just before midnight, and his clothes replaced on his body, which was then dumped."

"How do you work that out?" Findlater

stared at Montgomerie with cold, keen eyes. Donoghue too had discovered a new alertness.

"Because I visited Tiny Jardine on Sunday. I told him about McCusker."

The ensuing silence was similar to that which follows the sudden slam of a door in a large house which is supposed to be empty save for the listener. Finally Findlater spoke. Turning to Elka Willems he said, "Don't minute that."

There was another silence.

"I don't know why I went. I told him about McCusker when I became angry after he offered me a bribe."

There was a third silence, broken when Donoghue said, "Do you know what you've done?"

"You mean that this is the end of the line for DC Montgomerie? Yes, I've thought of that."

"Probably you're right but that isn't up to anybody here," replied Donoghue. "What I mean is that through your actions you have caused a man to lose his life. You even had opportunity to tell me this when you saw McCusker being taken from the safe house. We would have been able to save him."

In the moments which followed Montgomerie noticed for the first time that the clock on the wall of Findlater's office had a barely audible tick. Then he said. "I hadn't thought of that."

10.06 a.m. Ray Sussock drove off the ferry and parked the car near the harbour. He cashed a cheque at a bank and walked along Rothesay front to a hotel and took breakfast. He ordered the full spread with two eggs and heavy on the mushrooms and washed it down with a gallon of tea. Feeling more like a human being, he drove to the southern tip of Bute and knocked up a bemused Mrs. Spicer. "No, I can't tell you what it's about. I'm sorry, madam. Please hurry, I'd like to catch the next ferry."

10.13 a.m. Montgomerie was first in the room. Tex started to go for him but backed down when he saw Findlater's bulk looming behind Montgomerie. Donoghue was third, then three constables, then Elka Willems. One constable remained outside the front door of the house.

"The front door wasn't locked," said Montgomerie by way of explanation to Tiny

Jardine, who had suddenly lost all the colour from his face.

"What . . . how . . ." Jardine started to stutter. Montgomerie walked across the floor of the room to the hearth and picked up the branding irons. "I was afraid you would have destroyed them by now," he said. He took the irons over to Findlater, who examined them and then gave them to the constable, who left the house. There was a strong smell of disinfectant in the room and Montgomerie drew Findlater's attention to a recently applied area of plastering on the wall near the door.

"We'll probably find the bullet in there," said Findlater.

"Strong smell of cleaning agents, Tiny," said Montgomerie. "Been cleaning up some mess?"

"Wasn't the money good enough?" snarled Jardine.

"That won't work," said Donoghue calmly.

"So he's told you he came here, has he, asked for money?" Jardine pointed accusingly at Montgomerie.

"That's not quite what he said and I'd believe him before I'd believe you."

"I suppose you have a warrant?"

"Of course," replied Donoghue, tapping his jacket pocket. "We like to do these things properly. Would you like to see it?"

Tiny Jardine shook his head. Then he asked, "What is all this about anyway?"

"Feller called McCusker," said Montgomerie. "We found the body at Bishopbriggs this morning."

Tiny Jardine glared suddenly at Tex, who looked at the floor.

"What's the matter?" Donoghue asked. "Did you tell him to dump the body in the river or something?"

"I was tired, boss . . ."

"Shaddup!" snapped Tiny Jardine.

"It's always the little things that trip up the big ones," said Donoghue to Findlater, but loud enough for Jardine to catch it.

"I want my solicitor," said Jardine.

"He's in gaol," said Montgomerie.

"He's turned Queen's Evidence," said Findlater.

"Told us about the accounts of Deneave Holdings," said Montgomerie.

"Which we are presently reading with great interest," said Donoghue.

"The little rat," said Tiny Jardine.

Donoghue turned to Tex and casually asked, "Did you throw the murder weapon away too?"

"No, it's . . ." said Tex and then looked like he wanted to be some place else.

"You stupid bastard," sighed Tiny Jardine as he sank on to the settee.

Findlater ordered that the house be searched.

Elka Willems found Susie in a chair in the room at the end of the corridor labelled The Waterhole. She was nursing a not very full bottle of vodka and was sobbing gently. She looked like she'd been punched around the face a couple of times.

"Tiny did this?" asked the tall policewoman.

Susie nodded. Elka Willems's uniform didn't seem to concern her.

"For why?"

"Because I shot that guy."

"You shot him?"

"Aye, for to stop him screaming. He'd been screaming for hours, even through the gag he was screaming, and the smell when Tiny pushed the iron on to him . . . ugh!" The girl shuddered. "I couldn't stand it no longer so I went to where Tiny keeps his

303

guns and I got one and went right up to the guy and . . ."

"OK hen, OK. I think you've had enough, let me take this, eh?" There was a brief tug of war with the bottle but Susie finally let it go. "So where does Tiny keep his guns?"

"Over there." Susie pointed to a bar which ran across the far wall. There were a few glasses and a bottle standing on it. "It hinges up," she said.

"Is that where the murder weapon is, love?"

"No. I threw it in the pool. Tiny came at me so I ran and found myself next to the pool. I lobbed the gun in because I was afraid I'd shoot Tiny if I didn't chuck it away. Mind you, now I—"

"It would only have been worse for you. Do you mind if I put these on you?"

"They're not like the ones in the films."

"They're not, are they? These are handcuffs, leather, female prisoners for the use of."

Montgomerie and Donoghue stood by the edge of the swimming-pool. On the bottom of the pool underneath the diving-board was a .38 revolver. Despite the shimmering image of the gun both police officers could see that the hammer was cocked. Susie had come a lot closer to shooting Tiny Jardine than she had admitted, or had realized. Montgomerie slung the towel he was carrying across the rails of a jogging machine. He peeled off his jacket and unclipped his tie.

"What do you think my chances are, sir?" he asked.

"Of staying in the force? They're good, Montgomerie, they're very good, if you want to stay in. You didn't take the bribe and you did report the incident. But you've damaged yourself, you've got a lot of ground to win back before you can even dream of promotion. What happened to McCusker happened because of your stupidity and it's you that has to live with that, not the police force."

Donoghue walked back down the side of the swimming-pool. As he reached the far end of the pool he heard a loud splash behind him, as though Montgomerie had thrown himself at the water, rather than dived in. Donoghue walked into the main room of the house where Tiny Jardine and Tex stood each handcuffed to a police constable. He walked across the room, feeling in his jacket pocket as he did so, and then stopped in his tracks. He'd left his pipe on a wall in Bishopbriggs.

The trial of Susie Currie, the Jardine brothers and John Spicer took place in the High Court of Glasgow two months later, with psychiatric reports being requested in respect of one defendant. Susie Currie's plea of not guilty to murder was accepted by the Crown and she was sentenced to three years' imprisonment on the lesser charge of culpable homicide. Phil Jardine was sentenced to five years' imprisonment for fraud, Income Tax evasion and conspiracy to rob. Tiny Jardine was sentenced to ten years' imprisonment for conspiracy to rob, fraud, malicious wounding, assault to severe injury and offences under the Firearms Act. And John Spicer was dragged screaming from the dock, having been sentenced to be detained at Her Majesty's Pleasure.

GUIDE
TO THE COLOUR CODING
OF
ULVERSCROFT BOOKS

Many of our readers have written to us expressing their appreciation for the way in which our colour coding has assisted them in selecting the Ulverscroft books of their choice. To remind everyone of our colour coding— this is as follows:

BLACK COVERS
Mysteries

*

BLUE COVERS
Romances

*

RED COVERS
Adventure Suspense and General Fiction

*

ORANGE COVERS
Westerns

*

GREEN COVERS
Non-Fiction

MYSTERY TITLES
in the
Ulverscroft Large Print Series

Murders Anonymous	*Elizabeth Ferrars*
Don't Whistle 'Macbeth'	*David Fletcher*
A Calculated Risk	*Rae Foley*
The Slippery Step	*Rae Foley*
This Woman Wanted	*Rae Foley*
Home to Roost	*Andrew Garve*
The Forgotten Story	*Winston Graham*
Take My Life	*Winston Graham*
At High Risk	*Palma Harcourt*
Dance for Diplomats	*Palma Harcourt*
Count-Down	*Hartley Howard*
The Appleby File	*Michael Innes*
A Connoisseur's Case	*Michael Innes*
Deadline for a Dream	*Bill Knox*
Death Department	*Bill Knox*
Hellspout	*Bill Knox*
The Taste of Proof	*Bill Knox*
The Affacombe Affair	*Elizabeth Lemarchand*
Let or Hindrance	*Elizabeth Lemarchand*
Unhappy Returns	*Elizabeth Lemarchand*
Waxwork	*Peter Lovesey*
Gideon's Drive	*J. J. Marric*
Gideon's Force	*J. J. Marric*
Gideon's Press	*J. J. Marric*
City of Gold and Shadows	*Ellis Peters*
Death to the Landlords!	*Ellis Peters*
Find a Crooked Sixpence	*Estelle Thompson*
A Mischief Past	*Estelle Thompson*

FICTION TITLES
in the
Ulverscroft Large Print Series